FLOATERS

A NOVELLA

GARRETT BOATMAN

Let the world know:
#IGotMyCLPBook!

Crystal Lake Publishing
www.CrystalLakePub.com

CRYSTAL LAKE PUBLISHING RECOMMENDATIONS

Midnight Horror Show by Ben Lathrop
Lilitu: The Memoirs of a Succubus by Jonathan Fortin
The Final Cut by Jasper Bark
Where the Dead Go to Die by Mark Allan Gunnells and Aaron Dries

WELCOME
TO ANOTHER

CRYSTAL LAKE PUBLISHING
CREATION

WELCOME TO ANOTHER CRYSTAL LAKE PUBLISHING CREATION.

Thank you for supporting independent publishing and small presses. You rock, and hopefully you'll quickly realize why we've become one of the world's leading publishers of Dark Fiction and Horror. We have some of the world's best fans for a reason, and hopefully we'll be able to add you to that list really soon.

To follow us behind the scenes (while supporting independent publishing and our authors), be sure to join our interactive community of authors and readers on Patreon (https://www.patreon.com/CLP) for exclusive content. You can even subscribe to all our future releases. Otherwise drop by our website and online store (www.crystallakepub.com/). We'd love to have you.

Welcome to Crystal Lake Publishing—Tales from the Darkest Depths.

For Roberta, my darling wife and constant muse

1

THE SWELLS WERE DRUNK. There were three of them. Young toffs, their fine suits looking worse for wear after a night of East End carousing. Still joking and pulling at a shared bottle as the wherry made its way upriver. Midnight was long past and dawn too far off for Jenkins' taste. Father Thames was in a foul mood. Night was thickest on the Surrey side, the glassworks and wharves invisible behind the greasy banks of fog. On the City side, the electric lights of the Temple Pier and Victoria Embankment glowed through the murk like will-o'-the-wisps.

Despite the dark and the fog, old Clarence Jenkins, who had been dipping his oars in these muddy waters since before the Great Stink, knew every dock and water stair on both sides of the river and could find his way blindfolded. He loved the dear old cantankerous river in all its lights and liked to think of it as his, but lately the relationship had soured. He wanted to attribute his failing affection for the river to age. He was getting on and the damp aggravated his rheumatism.

But that wasn't it. Distrust had set in.

Though it had never happened to him personally, he imagined it was like knowing your wife's cheating

1

on you and not being able to prove it but deep down knowing. Not that Beth would ever and who would have her?

His oars dipped and rose and dipped and the wherry glided in little sprints. Temple Pier's lights grew brighter.

Lately, there was gossip, tales of disappearances. A colleague, Tom Button, had gone missing last week, along with the two couples he was rowing over from Southwark to Waterloo Pier. Vanished. No bodies found. The boat was discovered mired in the mud past Blackfriars. A gentleman's coat and a lady's purse were all that was found of his fare. Clarence had seen the police in their steamers and longboats out searching, plying their lamps over the water. They told the watermen to take care. Of what they declined to say. Only keep a sharp eye and if you see anything unusual do not investigate but pull hard till you've left whatever it was behind.

Had some strange fish inhabited the Thames? Some behemoth from the ocean's depths trying its luck in fresher waters? He'd once seen a whale beached at Gravesend, reeking worse than the old Thames in summer before Bazalgette built the embankment and diverted the sewage through his maze of brick tunnels. People had come from miles to wonder at the size of the thing. Looking across the black surface heaving beneath the drifting fog, he shuddered. No, it wasn't old age or too long acquaintance. Lately, a change had come upon the river.

Though it was summer, the nights were cold. And though the flocks of swans that greeted ships in centuries past were greatly reduced, they were still occasionally encountered. In the past week, Clarence had seen not one.

The hanging lantern swayed with the movement of the boat. The toffs' slurred banter accompanied the near-imperceptible dip of the oars. Apparently, the youngest of the three had been pickpocketed.

"It was her pimp that lifted your wallet," the somewhat older, yellow-vested gentleman said.

"She was no prostitute!" insisted the hatless youth. His cravat was loose, his slurred syllables testament to his inebriation.

His fellows rolled their eyes and shared a knowing look.

"I suppose you'll compose a villanelle about her virtue?" said the hook-nosed sporting lad.

"How much did you lose?" said the first, either to distract from the other's tease or to further taunt.

"Four guineas." The injured youth presented a pugilistic visage to his mates.

The others' low whistle carried in the fog.

"You could have bought all the whores in the hall with that," Yellow-vest ventured.

"Not to worry. His dad will replace it," Hook-nose illumed.

"I'll not be telling Father."

"I should think not. Chalk it up to experience. Never carry more than you need and always ask for credit."

"I don't think his girl would take credit."

"She wasn't my girl." The beleaguered youth was getting annoyed.

"I should say not."

The topic exhausted, the sporting gentleman

produced a cigarette case. Smokes were selected, the case returned. Lighting their cigarettes was no mean feat in the damp.

Jenkins glanced over his shoulder. The lamps of Temple Pier glowed brighter. Though no more than a dozen yards away, the pier itself remained invisible behind the fog.

He was turning the boat when an oar snagged on something. He gave a tug. It wasn't unusual to come upon refuse, rags, dead dogs. Once a half-submerged horse floated past. Whatever it was, the boat stalled and veered back into the channel.

"What the blazes?"

"What's wrong, Guv?"

A hand came over the gunnel. The youngest toff screamed. Yellow-vest ill-advisedly stood, rocked the boat, and staggered. Hook-nose half rose to grab his mate, further upsetting the boat, and Yellow-vest fell into the water.

Clarence saw none of this. He was mesmerized by what followed the hand.

The face that rose above the gunnel was pocked and noseless and pale as an alewife's belly. One eye was white as fog, the other was missing.

Clarence unshipped an oar and slammed it into the boarder's face. Hand and face disappeared. Yellow-vest was screaming, splashing frantically. The gentleman's hand grasped the gunnel and his face appeared for an instant, eyes brimming with horror. Then, as if yanked back into the water, he was gone.

Fares forgotten, Clarence's hands shook as he tried to return the oar to its lock, missed, got it. Then he was rowing as if the devil were coming for him. But other

FLOATERS

hands were on the gunnels, bloated faces glowing in the luminous fog.

***

Beneath a bridge on a cobbled path beside a canal, Ol' Daniel Tobin raised a bottle to the dead and sang into the billowing fog:

No more we'll go a sailing,
We'll round the Horn no more,
So it's drop the anchor laddies,
And haul the boats ashore.

For it's Tyburn that awaits me,
The mast a gallows tree,
The rigging is a single rope,
The knot no sailor's be.

For it's to the tree against the gale
That's roaring in my heart,
And on the morn hauled up the mast
I must this world depart.

But spare no sorrow laddies,
Drink up while you may,
And sing a capstan shanty,
And salute the breaking day.

So tip the jug and drink up boys,
And see me on my way,
As I shall up the Tyburn mast,
and dance until I sway.

So reef the mains'l laddies,
And haul the boats ashore,
The ship we'll leave at anchor,
We'll sail the sea no more.

His song done, Ol' Dan drank and smacked his lips and, his gleaming eyes seeing bygone days, held his bottle high and danced a jig. But the stones were damp, and he slipped and fell with a booming splash and the water closed over his head. He came up sputtering and rapidly sobering and reached for the greasy curb. But a hand clenched his leg and another his belt and hauled him under where pale faces grinned. His scream rose in bubbles as they dragged him down.

2

THE KNIVES AND BELTS were out. Will Tagget brandished a big chopper as he circled Bill Drummond.

It was all prearranged. Will and his Lambeth Walk Lads had agreed to meet up with the Drury Lane Gang on the Lambeth side of Westminster Bridge where, as per custom, insults that never failed to provoke were exchanged and the gangs would give each other what for. The row wasn't so much about territory—a bridge and a river divided them after all—as about bragging rights.

Bill Drummond of the Drury Lane Monkeys kept his only slightly smaller blade steady. Body crouched, elbow bent, his beady eyes watched for an opening. Drummond was a good bladesman, Will gave him that. But Will's grim grin proclaimed he was better.

Across the water, the half-hour boomed from Westminster. The clock tower and House of Commons were lost in fog. All that marked the far shore were the lamps of the Victoria Embankment. Even here, on the Albert Embankment behind St. Thomas, the fog was so thick you could scarcely make out the figures that silently circled and thrust and occasionally hissed as a blade nicked flesh.

7

Will noted with contempt that a couple of the Drury Lane crew wore coats buttoned to the collar. His boys wouldn't be caught dead wearing armor. They'd showed up in their best shirts, as if on the way to pick up their girls for an evening at the Victoria. Will wore a dark-blue neckerchief, neatly knotted, that did duty for collar as well as tie. Save for the scrape of feet, the occasional snick of connecting blades and the lap of water against the Embankment wall, the night was eerily quiet.

Bill Drummond swept in low and quick. Will leaned back just far enough to avoid the blade, then, as Drummond's hand withdrew, followed with his own swipe. But Drummond knew what was coming and slipped just far enough right so the blade missed and he was in position to take another stab at Will. So the dance went. In earnest now, belts swinging from one hand while the knife hand feinted and stabbed. As serious a task as breaking into a swell's house in an unfamiliar neighborhood. The object was not to snuff your rival—the law didn't take kindly to having to work—but to draw blood.

A scream startled them both. Will knew it instantly for one of his. Hulking Tim Peck who was fourteen but big for his size and learning the ropes. His first thought was one of the Drury Lane rotters had stuck him, but then he saw the figures shambling up the water stairs.

Though it was hard to see in the dim light—the lamp posts were invisible, so the Embankment lights seemed to float in the fog like Chinese lanterns—it was obvious something was very out of place. For one thing, the interlopers—there appeared to be five or six of them—were coming up from the river and he'd heard no dip of approaching oars. For another, they moved with a shambling gait, thick silhouettes bent, heads jutting forward, arms reaching. There was a woman among them. He couldn't make out her face, but she appeared to be hindered by her dress which clung to her legs as if she had just emerged from the river.

The fray abandoned, those nearest the newcomers backed away. Will moved forward, Bill Drummond beside him.

"What the deuce?" Will hissed when he saw what had crashed their party. He liked to see fear in others—it caused hesitation, and hesitation was deadly in the heat of action. As for himself, he'd outgrown the indulgence at six, cast it off as impractical and inexpedient. So he was appalled to feel the icy chill of the foreign emotion sluicing through his stomach, the skin on his back crawling.

Tim was down, one of the creatures hunched over him, knees straddling his body, mangy head twisting close to his face. Grisly sounds like soft bones crunching and old wallpaper ripping from plaster reached his ears. Will stopped when he saw through parting fog what the thing was doing. It was eating Tim!

Eating him alive!

As he watched, for the first time in memory at a loss for action, the thing shook its head like a mastiff throttling a cat and a long strip of Tim's face ripped free. Blood from the meat and water from its sopping mane sprayed the air. It threw back its head and wolfed down the meat like a hungry dog. The eyes rolled back in its head were white, covered in milky cataracts. As if it sensed his presence, it looked straight at him and, with a show of bloody teeth, hissed a warning before returning to its hideous repast.

The enormity of what he was seeing overwhelmed Will, and for a moment that stretched to eternity, he was like anybody else reduced to the lowest common denominator of human existence—fight or flight. Terror loosened his knees.

He shook off the horror. Deal with that later. A friend was down. Never mind his assailant was something out of a nightmare. He had to be dreaming. Couldn't possibly be awake. He started forward.

A hand on his arm: Bill Drummond.

It should have done his heart good to see Drummond's face as pale as flour, but he didn't have time for the luxury. Tim was bleeding out—if he was even alive.

***

The survivors retreated to an abandoned warehouse. Though the big quayside doors kept the fog at bay, the air was thick with damp. Someone lit a candle, and they picked their way across a stone floor slick with moss. The brick walls were furred with mold, the iron pillars red with rust. There was little in the way of debris. Everything has its use. Even household waste is sorted for paper, rags, and metals on London's refuse wharves before being pulverized and incinerated in destructors. Here everything the owners hadn't sold had long been harvested—even smashed barrels and crates served for firewood on a wintry night.

The air reeked of river. Will's shirt reeked of something fouler. He'd tangled with one of their ghastly attackers.

The melee ended in a struggle between the living and the dead. Will Tagget was a practical man and seeing daily the cons pulled on gullible shills and the chicanery politicians perpetrated on the public, he was also a deeply skeptical one. And while he gave no credence to the ghosts, vampires or other supernatural whatnots that appeared in the penny bloods, and while he would like to believe in a nurturing God who had the well-being of his lambs in his heavenly heart, his personal observation of the brutal living conditions of London's have-nots coupled with the equally brutal exploitation by the haves discouraged any such belief. In his experience, "father figures" exploited their wards for personal benefit and beat them or cast them off when no longer productive. His stance was if something appeared improbable, assume it was a con until examination proved otherwise. What they'd encountered tonight defied all credence, yet the evidence of his senses argued for belief.

Their uncanny animation smacked of witchcraft. Their cheesy flesh came off in your hand but slowed them not at all. Some were missing eyes, as if fish had nibbled them out on the Thames' muddy bottom. One was missing its jaw, another lacked a foot so that it lurched hideously but failed to fall. And they were quick. For all their shambling and seeming blindness, when you moved in to strike, they caught your hand or wrist and didn't let go. And they were strong. Chauncey Bellows sported a broken wrist to attest to their strength. But it was the water that cinched it for Will. When he'd slit the throat of the creature feasting on Tim, dark blood had gushed out of the wound. But in afterthought, since it was eating Tim's face, that might have been Tim's blood. He'd half beheaded it, his blade ripping through muscle and cartilage so that the throat opened like a second mouth and the head lolled back connected by spine. It hadn't collapsed but continued chomping even when its head came to rest on one shoulder. But when he ducked beneath the dripping arms of another attacker and ripped a swath of belly, sternum to navel, it wasn't blood that spilled from the great wound along with ropy coils of guts but water. And as the putrid water rained down upon the Embankment pavers and the figure deflated, it did not fall but continued shambling forward, arms outstretched, fingers grasping, jaws chomping.

They'd inflicted damage, managed to hack the heads off two of them, but nothing stopped the creatures. The headless bodies kept advancing. The heads, lolling on their ears, kept chomping, as if possessed of a demonic hunger that knew no sating. And though they'd outnumbered their attackers twelve to six, they'd lost three of their own: Tim and two of the Drury Lane squids, Lem Carey and Jonas Falk. Worse, they'd been unable to reclaim their dead, but had left them where they lay while retreating with their tails between their legs.

They gathered in what had been a supervisor's office. The desk was still there, a big steel thing too heavy to move, and wooden file cabinets tipped on their sides, their drawers missing, for firewood most likely, the papers taken for kindling. A length of black stove pipe hung from a wall; the pot-bellied stove that once warmed his nibs while the workers looked to their labor to warm themselves was missing, probably adorning some parlor or shop. An old mattress with a piece of rotten sailcloth for a blanket lay in a corner amongst a clutter of empty gin bottles, but no sign of the tosser.

Will's legs hadn't shaken this bad since he'd gone ten rounds with Bob Dundee. Though Dundee had two stone and nearly a foot on him, he'd won that battle. This one he'd lost. Looking around at the survivors' faces in the candlelight, he wondered if his face was as white as theirs.

"Deaders," he hissed.

"What's that?" Drummond said.

"The fuckers were dead."

"Not possible. Lepers . . . had to be."

"Then why didn't they bleed?"

Drummond had no answer to that.

"Whadda we do?" Ralph Bailey wanted to know. Ralph was a Lambeth Lad, and his face was as white as Drummond's. "Go to the police?"

"No coppers!" Frank Peck said, slashing the air with his still dripping blade for emphasis. A line of droplets splattered Ralph's face. Frowning, Ralph wiped them with his sleeve: though bloodless the drops reeked of guts and offal. Frank was Tim's older brother. Far from the pallor of other faces, his was beet red. He'd beheaded one of the deaders and chopped its hands off. They'd had to pull him off another when it became apparent they were fighting a losing battle.

Drummond looked about to say something, thought better of it. Frank still wielded his dripping cutter and looked anxious to hack something.

Will held Frank's gaze until he had the lad's attention. "No coppers," he agreed. He turned to Bill

Drummond. "They'd never believe us. Throw us in the jug. We've got to warn ours."

"I gotta go back and get Tim," Frank Peck said. He gripped the haft of his eight-inch chopper as if daring anyone to try and stop him.

"We will. But we need more bodies and bigger knives." Will looked at his own chopper, still seeing the deader advancing even as it trod its own guts. He turned to Chauncey. "Get the word out. Meet at"—he eyed the Drury Lane monkeys—"you know where. We'll go back for Tim with an army. I got a feeling there's more of them deaders coming."

"What's that smell?" One of the Drury Lane boys, potato-faced Alvin Pott, wrinkled his bulbous razzo.

Will had attributed the smell to the stink rising from their clothes and dripping from their knives. But the stench had gotten stronger. He looked around. Water was seeping through the plaster, trickling down the walls. Cracks appeared and the inundation increased, rivulets spilling onto the floor, reeking as only the Thames can when heavy rains flush the city's sewers into its channels. The water spread over the flagstones, lapped against their shoes.

Harry Hodd, who stood nearest to the big window that separated the office from the work floor, said in a hushed voice, "We got company, Will."

Coppers! was Will's first thought. But when he looked out, his scrotum tightened and the hairs on his neck prickled as if a cold skeletal finger had touched him there.

Bloated shadow shapes emerged from the darkness. Grasping hands clawed the air. Pocked, fish-pale faces turned as one, as if they'd singled him out for attention. Several panes were missing from the window and Will heard the *slop-slop* of wet feet advancing. He gagged on the reek that billowed through the missing panes and rose from the seeping floor.

A sharp cracking sound startled him as the plaster split open behind him and water gushed from the wall as if the warehouse were submerged and the river was pouring in. Water ran over the tops of their shoes. The stench was unbearable.

Brandishing his blade, Frank Pike started for the door. Will put a hand on his arm.

"We gotta go," Bill Drummond said.

The deaders were between them and the way they'd entered the warehouse on the quayside. Holding Frank back by sheer force, Will saw their numbers had increased. There appeared to be a dozen at least. They were outnumbered.

"Come on. I know another way," he said and, shoving through the door, took off in the opposite direction. On the street side, there was a boarded-over section where someone had lifted a door. They'd smash their way out if they had to.

Water seeped up through the floor slabs. The virulent reek of shit and rotting weeds burned his nostrils.

They almost made it.

A hand grabbed Will and spun him round, slammed him against the wall.

"Gotcha, you little shite!"

A bullseye lantern momentarily blinded him. The harsh aroma of cheap cheroot billowed into his face. The broad sneering countenance came into focus. Mutton chops. Hard eyes beneath a bowler.

Detective-Inspector Brice Lock, Lambeth Division. The Inspector had him by his shirtfront; his other hand squeezed his wrist, banged his knife hand against the bricks. He thought about wrestling his hand loose and using his knife on the copper, but only in passing. There were rules to the games they played with coppers. While it was rare sport to stuff a constable head-first down a manhole, you didn't kill one or even stab him. Everybody got a good drubbing coming up on the streets; it toughened you up, taught you to give as well as take. But if killing a constable was crossing a line, killing a Detective-Inspector was a certain death warrant. He dropped his blade.

Lock had two uniformed police constables with him. Will knew them both. Dennis Foley, a few years his senior and from his neighborhood, was grudgingly respected. A former member of Lambeth Polytechnic Boxing Club, Foley was more than a match for any three of the local hoodlums. Foley and the Lambeth Walk Lads had a tacit agreement: so long as he didn't catch them in the act, they would pass on opposite sides of the street.

The other copper, a lanky whippet with big feet and big hands, was a transfer from H Division. Will didn't know his name but heard nothing good about him. Hailing from Whitehall, he thought he was tougher than Lambeth boys. That got him tossed through a plate-glass window and he'd been out of work three weeks. Since one shilling was docked from an officers' pay for every day they were sick, the story fetched a rare smile from Will when it reached his ears.

Foley had Frank by the scruff. Will prayed Frank would drop his chopper. Foley twisted his wrist and the weapon skittered into the darkness. Whippet pursued the Lambeth Lads and Drury Lane monkeys, but being outnumbered he quickly returned.

"They got away," he groused as if actually disappointed.

"Never mind. We've got the ringleader." Lock leaned in close so his words burst moist in Will's face. "We found your dead mate. You're in for it now."

"You'll be in for it if we don't all get out of here!" Will couldn't resist leaning forward till he was nose to nose with the Inspector. Lock was taller so he stood on his toes.

Lock released Will's shirtfront and raised his hand to backhand him, but Foley interrupted.

"Inspector, look!"

Lock followed the constable's gaze.

To the Inspector's credit, he didn't flinch when he saw what was bearing down on him, but greeting the newcomers with snarling teeth, he drew his Webley Bulldog and fired into one misshapen face and then another. His third shot went wild as he was borne to the ground by two others, who fell upon him as more dropped to their knees and joined in the carnage.

Will's blood ran cold. He saw what they were doing to the Inspector—they were eating him as they had Tim, stooping to bite his cheeks and arms, tearing his clothes, ripping bloody strips from his carcass and cramming them into their maws as if they were ravenous.

Will grabbed Frank's arms, pulled him out of Foley's grasp and ran. Whitechapel, armed only with truncheon and whistle, beat them to the open door. Foley tried to reach his superior, but Lock was surrounded. Hands ripped his clothes, teeth savaged his throat. Others attacked Foley. Nails raked his uniform. His truncheon cracked on wrists and hands and faces as he fought his way free.

Outside in the swirling fog, Whitechapel was nowhere in sight. Will and Frank ran in the cobblestone street past the warehouse's long façade. Rapid footfalls came up behind them. Will shoved Frank ahead, growled, "Go!"

Frank glanced back. Will said, "It's okay. Gather the troops."

Frank sped off. Will hung back. Foley grabbed him from behind but didn't stop. Tired of people pawing his shirt, Will slapped the hand away.

"What were those things?"

Any other time, Foley's pallor would have put a smile on Will's face, but Tim was dead. And Detective-Inspector Lock. The police would be seeking blood for an Inspector's murder. No way they were going to believe a rookie or a gang member! Foley and Whitechapel would likely lose their jobs for not giving their lives for their superior—never mind that Lock was the one with the revolver.

"Deaders," Will said, keeping stride with the taller constable.

"Dead—?"

"Not living, snuffed. They came out of the river."

"That explains the water, the wet clothes, but dead?" He shook his head.

"For fuck's sake, didn't you smell them? And they keep coming. You can't stop them."

"The first one DI Lock shot in the head dropped."

"Did it? That's good to know. I didn't stop to watch."

Constable Foley stopped him. They were among houses now, still in the middle of the foggy, deserted street.

"You've got to come with me to the station," Foley said. His normally confident voice cracked with uncertainty.

"Right, and swing for Lock's murder!"

"I'll vouch for you."

"A hooligan's gonna be a better fit for Lock's death than deaders coming out of the river."

Foley grabbed Will's shirt as he started to leave. Will spun, planted his foot squarely between the rookie's legs and, while Foley was doubled over, fled into the night.

***

With an entrance on one street and an exit on another, the public house made a convenient meeting place. The can—in his day an artful forger of snide coin and a former Wandsworth inmate, who, consequently, was no friend of John Law—for a small but steady enumeration, was the soul of discretion and sure to make a ruckus easily heard through the thin walls should said Law come nosing.

The tap was too soft to be made by any cocked-hatted Lambeth Lad. Will opened the door, glanced down the papered hall to the right and left to ascertain they were alone, then pulled her in.

Kate was tall as he. Which, as he was a little under average height and wiry—a natural for fanlight jumping and drainpipe climbing—made her a tad tall for a girl. Her yellow dress was out-of-season, more appropriate for a summer day than this fog-damp night; but it was her favorite color and matched wonderfully her straight blond hair. The blue sash around her slim waist, along with the blue shoes he'd filched for her, added a touch of razzle.

He no sooner closed the door than she was in his arms, or would have been if he'd not caught her and held her off.

"Don't want to ruin your dress."

She flashed him a worried smile, wrinkled her nose when she caught the whiff off his shirt, leaned in and kissed him anyway. She stood back, looked him over for damage.

"I'm all right." He meant to sound annoyed—as he would be at anyone else rude enough to show concern over his well-being—but was secretly pleased with her attention.

"I heard about Tim. Is it true?"

Will returned to the two cane-back chairs—with a small bar table the only furniture in the room—sat. He nodded. "Tim's dead."

Even as he said it, he wondered if it were true—if Tim was truly dead.

Guts spilled and the creature still moving . . . heads lolling on the Embankment . . . chomping . . .

Kate lowered herself into the opposite chair, frowned. "You've ruined your shirt."

"Not my blood," he said.

Normally he would have delivered the line with a nonchalant indifference guaranteed to make a listener eager to hear the details of his latest caper—eager enough to stand him a round before the telling began. But the anger simmering behind his clenched teeth forced the words out in a growl.

Kate's grey eyes were questioning. "Tim's?"

He nodded.

"Tell me."

He told her. Kate was tough. He didn't sugar-coat the story. If the devil was coming for you, it was better to know he was coming and get ready to meet him straight on than have him sneak up on you unawares.

"And something else," he said, pouring himself a whiskey. His hand was shaking. He forced himself to calm it.

"What?"

"Lock said 'mate.' Said he'd found our dead 'mate.'"

"And?"

"We left three dead on the Embankment."

3

LONDON IS A CITY of rivers. Besides the Thames, there exist its many tributary creeks and rivers, most of them culverted and pressed into service as sewers for the great metropolis. The River Fleet flows under Holbein and Fleet Street and emerges as a drainage outlet in the embankment wall beneath Blackfriars Bridge. The Rivers Tyburn and Westbourne and the Effra in Southwark suffered similar fates as the population bourgeoned and the offal pouring into the Thames became insufferable. But a few open waterways emptying into the Thames remain—the Regents Canal, the Limehouse Cut and, farther east, the River Lea.

On the day following the attack on the Lambeth Lads and the Drury Lane Gang and the death of Detective-Inspector Lock, the fog lifted and the afternoon warmed enough for a few families to venture to Victoria Park to picnic and to row on the boating lake.

One family consisting of a young father and mother, a baby boy in a pram and a little girl in a blue dress and white bonnet brought some bread along and the girl was feeding a swan through the railing of the low fence separating the path from the boating lake.

The boy in the pram was sitting up watching his sister and laughing with delight as the swan dipped its graceful neck to pluck the bread floating on the water when the bird was suddenly yanked beneath the surface. The boy gave a cry, the girl started back in horror.

On the lake, boaters turned to see why the child was screaming when a pair of waterlogged hands gripped an oar and upset the boat. Other hands dragged first one then another of the boaters into the water.

Two brothers bicycling on the Regent's Canal towpath came upon a man in soaking clothes. As the man was fat and blocked the path, they had no choice but to stop. The older brother stopped well before the encounter, but the younger, newer to cycling and not yet adroit at the art of braking, almost ran into the man, and seeing his pocked and swollen face and milky eyes, veered before the reaching hands could grasp him. Unfortunately, he veered the wrong way and splashed into the canal where anxious hands thrust from the water received him and pulled him under.

Stunned by the sight of his brother's reception and the fat man moving toward him with surprising speed, the older brother just had time to turn his bike and sprint off screaming at the top of his lungs.

All over London Town where water met land, such occurrences were common. From the Limehouse quaysides to Battersea Park Pier, workers and pedestrians were attacked. And by and by, as reports circulated from precinct to precinct and what seemed like the ravings of mass hysteria gained credence and journalists and city administrators demanded answers, the police could no longer deny something monstrous was afoot.

***

He was being followed.

The word was out: the law was looking for him for Lock's murder.

Unable to return to his kip—not that the slugs knew its location, but they were thick in the streets around the Walk—Will passed most of the day in a shed behind the Lambeth Workhouse. When the bread and cheese Kate gave him ran out and a bleary sun hung over the Nine Elms Gas Works, he ventured forth.

He didn't know how many of his own lads were free. He suspected some of them might be picked up for questioning or tossed in the hole till they talked—which they wouldn't. But he'd left it to Kate to spread the word to the boys to invite all the hooligan gangs to a meeting. A tall order and make no mistake, as some would think it beneath them to meet with the Lads, while others nursed dreams of revenge. He asked Kate to convey the importance of diplomacy to his emissaries, an art he'd never mastered himself. But with a common deadly enemy in their midst, it was important they put aside their differences and postpone vendettas for a future date.

Kate and the Lambeth Gals would do some persuasion of their own, try to work through the hooligans' girlfriends to convince their men to put grudges on hold and meet. They'd have a harder time convincing the female members of rival gangs; he'd seen them brawl and, if anything, their fights were far more vicious than their male counterparts, consisting not of face-scratching and hair-pulling but of good straightforward punching and blocking that would make a prizefighter proud. Several were proficient with a straight razor.

Now he was being followed. He glanced back, feeling exposed, but saw nothing as he passed the glassworks' long brick exterior. He doubted it was his imagination. You come up on the street, you develop a sixth sense when something's not right. He was being followed and make no mistake.

He turned a corner, ducked into a doorway, waited, chopper in hand.

When no one passed, he emerged, turned left—and walked into Police Constable Dennis Foley.

Foley had his knife hand in an iron grip in an instant. Though he remained tense, ready for anything, Will didn't move. He was more than handy with his fists but no match for the Lambeth boxing champ three years running.

Most coppers' heads were weak and you could kid your way out of a tight spot. If you were on lookout while your mates were cracking a crib, you could offer to go look and thereby warn them to grease off. Or, so long as you didn't have the swag on you, if you got caught coming off a roof or hanging in an alley, tell him you thought you heard something and, suspecting some fanlight jumper, you thought you'd investigate. But not Foley. Coming up in the same neighborhood as Will, he knew all the dodges.

"You're out of uniform," Will said. It was true: instead of his dark-blue Melton togs, white 137 L on his collar, Brunswick star glinting on his helmet, the rookie wore a grey waistcoat over a white shirt, a herringbone flat cap and the corduroy trousers of a working stiff. As was ever the case, Foley's aggressive mustache was betrayed by his kindly eyes. "Why are you following me?"

"I was suspended."

Will saw how Foley's superiors must have taken his story. "They didn't believe you. And now you want me to back your story."

"I'm not taking you in."

"You still haven't answered my question: Why are you following me?"

Foley looked disgusted. "Cops ain't doing anything. They're gathering evidence. Lord Mayor's pressuring the Commissioner for answers, the Commissioner's pressuring the forensics guy from the City police and he's got constables out looking for bodies but there are none. They all disappear into the water."

"What's that got to do with me?"

"I grew up on the next block over from you. I know the Lads have got their ears to the street and know what's what before the sergeant's finished the morning muster." He paused, looked Will levelly in the eye and released his hand, trusting Will wouldn't use the chopper on him. "I've heard you've called for a meeting. I want to be there."

Will eyed him right back. Where Will, being averse to regular hours, reading—other than the *Illustrated Police News* and penny bloods—and sitting indoors for any length of time without a beer in one hand and a cheroot in the other, pursued his education on the street, Foley attended public school before joining the constabulary. Still, they came from the same neighborhood, shared the same neighbors, ate the same bangers and eel pies. Even attended the same church—Foley sitting in its pews listening to the old doffer and putting money into the offering box; Will making withdrawals from said box.

"No way."

"I'm coming. This is bigger than cop versus hooligan. We've got a common enemy. You've put differences aside."

"Can you?"

Foley stared at him.

"They'll want your blood."

"I'll take my chances."

***

At the Polytechnic—a philanthropic endeavor established for the betterment of London's working-class youth—members of rival gangs could come together and vent their hostilities in a refereed ring instead of with belts and shivs on the docks and back alleys. The Poly also offered evening vocational classes for young men and women who aspired to be more than van boys or costermongers or pickpockets and enter the world of clerks and mechanics.

Not that Will ever considered taking a trade! The thought of working for anyone for the paltry earnings apprentices made with fixed hours six days a week he found appalling as well as impractical—he could make more in one day than apprentices and costers made in a week and without rising at dawn to be at work by six. He wasn't opposed to rising early to intercept a beer delivery or other lucrative opportunity, but for the most part afternoons and evenings and the occasional night job suited him fine. On a good day, he could make upwards of fifteen shillings passing snide coin in shops and public-houses.

Still, he had to give Rev. Wills, the guiding light behind the Polytechnic's success, grudging respect. The man was a bona fide do-gooder, accepted everyone as they were. And if you came to Poly to watch a fight, you never had to listen to a sermon before a match. And there were free eats afterwards.

The climbing ropes and gymnastic rings of the multipurpose facility were raised out of the way and the parallel bars, vaulting horses, Indian clubs and barbells were moved to the sides. The spectator gallery above the gymnasium floor was deserted. It'd be full of observers on nights when the roped-off squares of the "rings" were set up and a half-dozen refereed matches going on at once.

The turnout was better than Will expected. Delegates from most of the North and South London gangs were present. Will was pleased to see the gangs' captains among their crews, loss of face being a greater humiliation than a busted head. Besides a significant showing of London's male gangs—the Dove Row Gang, New Cut Gang, Abby Street Boys, Clerkenwell Boys, East End Gang, Drury Lane Gang, the Elephant and Castle Gang in their finery, The Battersea Velvet Caps, the Wandsworth Scuttlers, the City Road Gang, the Green Gate Gang, the Golden Lane Gang, the Bow Commoners, and the Limehouse Reapers—Kate had managed to persuade quite a contingent of female gang members to attend. Chief among them were representatives from the Forty Elephants, the infamous, tough-as-they-come, all-female gang and counterpart of the Elephant and Castle Gang.

While the costermongers, laborers, mechanics, apprentices, and vagrants that made up the bulk of the gangs wore corduroy trousers secured by broad leather belts with heavy buckles that doubled as weapons (many a gentleman had lost his watch and wallet and a great deal of blood to those belts), the male Elephants were dapperly dressed in plaid jackets and bowlers. George Fish, their broad-shouldered, mutton-chopped leader, even sported a silk, cream-colored ascot.

The ladies of the Forty wouldn't dream of wearing the dresses they stole from posh High Street shops but sold them to pay for the finery they bought from the very shops from which they stole. Jane, their Queen, was regally dressed in a green silk gown that would not have looked out of place in a West End townhouse.

New Cut Beth had brought five of her girls. Razor Lil, Bill Drummond's girl, was present along with a few of hers. And a couple dozen other female toughs made a fearsome-looking group.

Police Constable Foley's presence caused a stir.

"What's he doing here?" Dirk Bogart, chief of the New Cut Gang smacked a shillelagh he took off an Irishman against his palm as if warming up for a head-splitter.

To his credit, Foley stepped forward and faced down the crowd. "I'm here to help," he said.

He was drowned out before he could continue.

"We don't need no stinkin' slop's help!"

"Fuckin' nerve!"

Will held up his hand. When the uproar quieted enough for him to be heard, he said, "By now you've all heard about the deaders coming up from the river and canals and grabbing folk."

"Floaters," a Green Gate Gang member said,

waving a newspaper. "The papers're callin' 'em 'floaters.'"

"Deaders, floaters, stinkin' river scum," Will said impatiently. "They ain't human. They killed Tim Peck—"

"And Lem Carey and Jonas Falk," Bill Drummond said.

"And Seth Barnett . . . and Kyle Harrington . . . and Millie Billingsley," others added.

It was obvious to Will the men and women gathered here had some idea of what they were dealing with.

"It's the rapture."

The speaker was Lyle Trilling, son of a Wandsworth minister, a man of the cloth who had a heavy hand with the belt. Trilling had found a better family in a gang, something a lot of the present company had in common. Though most of the men wore bowlers or caps, Trilling held his black velvet flat cap in his hands, as if remembering his manners in the presence of ladies.

"I'm no bible thumper," Will said, "but I don't think there's anything in the good book about flesh-eating dead people rising up from the river."

"Then it must be the water."

Heads turned. The speaker was a sandy-haired lad in a boiled white shirt, one of the Golden Lane Gang out of North London. Seeing him and two of his mates standing between and outnumbered by members of the City Road and Dove Row gangs—all of them fierce rivals—and no one drawing belts or knives gave Will hope they might pull this off.

"Satan knows with all the shite and rot and corpses

of animals and people thrown in, maybe the river's had enough!"

Foley spoke up. "It doesn't matter if it's the devil's doing or the river's," he said. This time no one interrupted him. "As Will said, these things kill. And they can't be killed. You can stop them if you chop them up." He looked to Will for confirmation. Will nodded. "And I imagine burning them would slow them down. Point is, if—as the papers are saying—everyone they kill joins their ranks, it won't be long till half of London is them preying on us."

He paused to let that sink in.

"But they're in the river, right?" said an Abby Street Boy. "And in the canals. How're we supposed to fight them? You don't expect us to swim, do you?"

That got a nervous laugh from a few. Even Bogart cracked a sour grin, his gold tooth glinting under the lights. Many a lad dreamed of knocking that tooth out of the big man's mouth, but few dared try. Will flashed on the image of Bogart's bowler floating on the tide while the shillelagh-wielding braggart took his chances on the muddy bottom. He dismissed the thought.

"If I may," Foley said in a commanding voice—a directive not a request. No one dissented. "As you observed, they're coming out of the river and the canals."

"Right," Will said when no one else would be caught agreeing with a copper.

"And we can't fight them in the water." That was a given. Though some of the lads present were excellent swimmers, among them were those who wouldn't think of wetting their feet unless there was profit in it. "So we need to draw them out."

"How?" several voices spoke at once.

"The question is where? The river's too open. They'd have the advantage. It's got to be somewhere we can contain them, surround them if possible."

"The West India Dock," Frank Peck said, itching for action.

"Too big. There's upwards of eighty acres of water in the basin."

"St. Katharine's then," said a Bow Commoner.

Will watched Foley. He figured he was thinking the same thing. St. Katharine's was smaller. The locks and swing bridge could be manipulated to trap the floaters in the basin and there were warehouses and walks on all sides.

"We're forgetting something," Foley said. "The canal."

It was true. According to the news out of North London, the creatures had infested the waters of the Regent's Canal.

"The Limehouse Basin," George Fish said, raising a ring-laden hand to his clean-shaven chin that protruded like a naked prominence between his bushy side-whiskers.

Foley nodded. "Small, contained by swing bridge and locks, and the Regent's Canal empties into it."

"How do we lure them in?"

"We use bait."

"What bait?"

Constable Foley's gaze encompassed everyone in the room. "You're looking at it."

4

ACROSS THE THAMES IN Westminster, the clock tower chimed the quarters. Big Ben followed tolling the hour. Nine o'clock. The river lapped against the water stair. It was less foggy tonight, but the humid air was fraught with chill.

They stood on the Vauxhall Stairs adjacent to Lack's Dock between the looming brick hulks of the Royal Flour Mills and a Gin and Vinegar distillery. The tide was in, the landing below the stair submerged. Descending beside the moss-covered wall, the slippery stone steps disappeared into the water, like an invitation to a drowning.

A crescent moon broke through the overcast and, for a minute, the river, the opposite embankment, the misty arc of the Vauxhall Bridge glowed like a luminous monochromatic painting. Then the moon retreated, plunging the river back into darkness.

"Now what?" Foley asked. He'd insisted on accompanying Will on his quest to capture a floater. Though Will would never admit it, he was glad of the company. It'd be nice to have someone pull the bogle off if one managed to get on top of you.

By way of answering, Will plunked another pebble into the water. When that didn't draw attention, he looked around, found a chunk of broken cobblestone and lobbed it into the drink. It sank with a loud *plunk* accompanied by a spout of water that fell back into the river with a splash.

Within seconds a head broke the surface.

The moon was withdrawn, the river darkly glittering, so all he saw was the silhouette of head and shoulders. The creature rose. Over the lapping of the tide against the stair, Will heard the water running off it in rivulets. Then the moon broke through the clouds, dimly illuminating the monstrosity that was even now making its way up the stair, its footfalls a wet *splat*, *splat*.

The creature was hunched over, long stringy hair matting her face. Her blouse and skirts clung to her bloated frame. The dress swished as the animated dead mounted the stair.

Will knew how slippery the stairs were. He imagined how precarious the thing's balance was. If he kicked it, it would probably fall; but he'd come here to capture one, not knock it back into the river. He backed away onto the dock, let it come for him.

It topped the stair, stepped onto the dock, and still it came, neither fast nor slow but inexorably, ponderously, as if it were a force of nature approaching—a cold front moving in, a thunderhead lowering over the city. Death with no promise of ease.

As if they'd drilled together, Will and Foley split up. Keeping to either side of the floater, they circled the horror, staying just out of reach. Tottering, grasping, swinging its arms in flailing arcs, it lurched now toward one, now toward the other, a watery growl gurgling up from its sodden lungs.

Will ducked under a flailing arm and drove his chopper into the bundle of nerves he knew to be housed in the armpit. As a boy, he'd once ducked under a bully's roundhouse and planted his fist in his pit. The bully howled, and, as if the arm had lost all strength, Will was pleased to see the arm hang useless at the bully's side. It had been a valuable lesson to the young hooligan, seeing that attacking what lay below the flesh was often more effective than whaling away at the outer skin.

The strike, which would certainly have rendered a normal person's arm immobile, seemed to have no effect on the creature. Will barely had time to withdraw his blade before the arm came down, nearly trapping his hand.

Foley's next move had more luck. While the beast focused on Will, the policeman moved in and drove his heel into the thing's ribs. It floundered, slipped and, arms pinwheeling, went down with a noise like wet laundry hurled to the street.

Before it could rise, Foley threw himself on its back, pinning it down. It bucked and heaved. Foley hung on. Ignoring its grasping hands, Will plunged his blade into its eye. He preferred fat blades but, at the moment, he wished his knife was a stiletto. The wedge of steel burst the eyeball but lodged against the bone of the socket.

The head thrashed, teeth chomped, as bloodless goo leaked from the ruptured eye. The thing's feet hammered the cement dock. Toes snapped with a loud crack.

Frustrated, Will plunged the blade into the woman's neck, wrenched it out severing cartilage, veins, nerves, and muscle. As on the previous night when he'd nearly beheaded the thing eating Tim Peck, the gaping wound did not prove fatal. Rather than expire, the creature redoubled its efforts to rise, to buck Foley from its back. Its hands continued to grasp, its teeth to gnash, its feet to drum a tattoo on the dock.

A sound caught Will's attention. A wet, watery noise. A splash followed by another.

From where he crouched, one knee pinning a writhing arm while Foley wrestled to draw the other to its side, he saw first one glistening face, then another, and a third rise into sight as three more of the creatures mounted the stair.

Foley followed his gaze, saw what he saw.

"We've got company. We have to go," he said.

"Hold on."

Desperate not to leave empty-handed, Will sawed at the thing's wrist. The grey meat parted as easily as wet cheese, but bone and tendon refused to yield to his blade.

The first of the bogles, eyeless and noseless, half its cheek eaten away, hair spidering its forehead, teeth and fingers working, stepped onto the dock.

"Will."

"Hold on!" More out of frustration than from any conscious design, Will placed his blade in the joint between the thing's hand and wrist and, putting his boot on the back of the blade, stomped. Hand and wrist severed with a grisly parting of tendon and bone. Will's blade grated against concrete.

Will jumped back as the hand scuttled toward him.

All three floaters were on the dock now—two men and a woman—water streaming from their sopping clothes. Perhaps the dead possessed a keen sense of smell, because blind or not, they advanced straight for the living. Behind them, two more emerged from the steps.

Will stabbed the hand, and with it writhing on his blade, he shouted, "Come on!" and sprinted for the narrow passage that ran between the factories to the street.

Foley fairly leapt from the creature's back and followed.

***

The severed hand—mottled and greenish-black and glistening with decay—was stronger than they would have thought and quite active. Dr. Simon, lecturer in pathology, specialist in bacteriology and director of St. Thomas' Medical School's clinical laboratory, tried placing the hand in a steel laboratory tray, but it scuttled out onto the zinc-topped table like a particularly nimble crab. Securing it with a pair of sturdy forceps, he relocated it to a deep glass bowl. Even then, discovering it couldn't simply crawl out, it took to leaping at the sides of the dish, and, as if the diabolical appendage were possessed of some fantastic learning ability, began trying to hook its pinky over the side. Apparently inexhaustible, it showed no abatement in its efforts to escape.

Dr. Simon looked up from the microscope, adjusted his wire rims. His majestic side-whiskers were considerably more hirsute than his bald pate which gleamed in the gaslight.

"Well?" Constable Foley asked impatiently.

Dr. Simon pursed his lips and focused his penetrating deep-green eyes on each of them before

37

answering. "Frankly, I've never seen anything like this. Every corpse has its own unique microbial signature," he said by way of preamble, "depending on its external and internal environment. In this case," he indicated the energetic hand, "the teeming microbial life present in the water of the Thames is more active than the usual insectile contribution to decomposition."

"Doctor . . ." Foley gave a sideways tilt of his head in Will's direction as if to indicate his companion's lack of understanding, though he appeared plenty lost himself at the doctor's language.

"Yes, I mean having been underwater for some time, I see no indication of flesh fly activity. No maggot larvae, no evidence of insectile colonization. But what's really strange . . ."

"Yes?"

The doctor hooked a thumb into the pocket of his waistcoat as he declaimed. "Ordinarily—always in fact—the cellular and microbial breakdown in a postmortem organism, be it insect or man, follows a predetermined course. Putrefaction is a process of self-digestion so to speak. Cellular walls, blood vessels, the intestines break down. Bacteria escapes from the gastrointestinal tract reducing soft tissue into gases, liquids, and salts. Oxygen depleted, aerobic bacterial species, which require oxygen to grow, shift to anaerobic ones, which feed not on oxygen but on the body's tissues, fermenting their sugars to produce the gases that cause bloating. The smell of putrescence attracts blowflies, which lay eggs, from which maggots hatch, which consume the rotting flesh. As Linnaeus noted, 'Three flies can consume a horse cadaver as rapidly as a lion.'"

He paused to let the enormity of what he'd said sink in, continued. "Now this—" The doctor thumped a knuckle against the glass, then started back when the hand leapt toward the sound. "Interesting," he said, returning his thumb to his waistcoat pocket. "As I was saying, this specimen does not follow the pathology of putrescence. The oxygen is depleted, the flesh is loosening from the frame beneath. Albeit far more tardily than normal, cellular structures are breaking down—hence the stench of putrefaction—but I see no evidence of anaerobic bacteria consuming the tissue."

"Look Doctor," Will said, anxious for action, his fingers drumming against his cords, "all I want to know is how do I kill it."

"Well, it's obvious you can't drown them." When Will and Foley didn't smile at his joke, Simon raised his bushy brows. "Let's see . . . " He turned to Foley. "You say your superior shot one and didn't slow it?"

Foley nodded.

"Makes sense. It's dead, blood's already leaked out of its deteriorating veins. It'd be like shooting a vegetable." He addressed Will: "And you severed the *brachial plexus*, the nerve bundle that runs from the spine through the armpit and down the arm. Unless your aim was poor—and I don't doubt your accuracy—the arm should, indeed, have been immobilized. Frankly," he said, raising his eyebrows again, "it's beyond my understanding. It will take some study and a complete specimen to determine the pathology."

Will glanced at a door at the end of the lab. It led to the dead house, euphemistically referred to as the "rose cottage" or—especially when discussing the deceased around children—"Rainbow's End." He wasn't especially superstitious—though he wouldn't go out of his way to step on a grave or walk under a ladder—but the thought of the room's tenants sleeping in drawers waiting their turn in the operating theatre gave him the shudders.

"We don't have time to study these . . . " he waved at the mottled hand, " . . . things. Again, I ask you, how do we kill it?"

Without further comment, the Doctor unstoppered a bottle he took from a shelf, half-filled a glass pipette and released the contents onto the back of the hand. The flesh bubbled, putrid steam rose. The hand danced about as if trying to shake off an attacker.

"Acid certainly works, but it would take a great quantity to dissolve a complete specimen. And I understand there are many more in our waterways."

Taking a scalpel from a metal drawer, Dr. Simon pinned the struggling hand to the bottom of the bowl and sliced off the index finger which he plucked from the bowl before the hand could hitch a ride on the forceps. He dropped the finger into the steel tray.

Will and Foley watched in fascination as the finger inched along and, encountering the wall, tried in vain to climb the smooth metal.

Leaving the finger to its ineffectual efforts, Simon went to a cabinet and returned with a can. Will didn't have to wait till the doctor unscrewed the lid and the fumes to hit him to know the canister contained kerosene: it read so on the label. Stepping up to the glass bowl, the pathologist administered a liberal splash over the hand, then extracted a Lucifer from his pocket and struck it. When he dropped the match, the hand ignited and raced about under a blur of flame.

Will caught the stench of burnt flesh. As the flesh blackened, the abomination redoubled its efforts to escape, as if driven by the primordial survival instinct. When the flames diminished, Simon splashed more kerosene on it. The flames ate the flesh until veins and muscle turned to ashes and the bones fell apart.

Simon poked at the bones with his forceps. "At least we know fire stops them," he said.

The fire, however, was not a complete victory. No longer bound by sinew, the individual bones quivered with ghoulish life.

5

FIRE AND PLAGUE. Certainly no strangers to London Town. But now fire consumes the docklands on both sides of the river, and the plague, newly risen from the Thames, threatens to put the Great Leviathan down once and for all. Fleeing citizens, their wagons and carts piled high with their worldly possessions, clog the thoroughfares, jam the bridges. No one takes to the river. The cry is away—away to the country, away to the north and west, away from the river and canals from which legions pour ravening for blood. Packed to bursting, citizens clinging to the roofs of the cars, trains depart the London stations—the Great Northern, The Great Western, the London and Northwestern, The Great Central—carrying their passengers to safety. They do not return.

As the army of the dead advances, those who fall beneath their bite rise and swell their ranks, consumed by an unspeakable hunger. In the City of London, the Lord Mayor has blocks of houses pulled down and torched in an effort to slow the advancing hoard. With some success: on Upper Thames Street, funneled between rows of blazing shops and dwellings, the dead are stopped when a mountain of wagons and crates and household furniture is set ablaze. Snarling, red

42

glare dancing in their eyes, glittering off their teeth, the creatures find their retreat cut off by a second blaze and so perishes hundreds of the river's damned. But the unrelenting contagion spreads.

While the dead seek only blood, another army takes advantage of the chaos. Boiling out of their warrens of poverty and rookeries of crime, the rabble of Whitechapel, Seven Dials, Shoreditch, Spitalfields, St. Giles, Limehouse and Clerkenwell swarm through London's affluent neighborhoods and shopping districts looting and burning. The Queen's Guard and Household Cavalry defend Buckingham Palace and St. James. At the Tower, the Yeoman Warders stand ready. The 9th Regiment of Foot flank the Bank of England and Royal Exchange. Ten thousand hastily recruited special constables bolster the police force. By moonshine from a distance, the city appears a hellscape of black and red.

***

Despite the new steam-powered conveyances, London is still a horse-driven town. Relied on for economy and transportation, over 300,000 horses live and work in London's precincts. Twenty-two thousand horses pull omnibuses every day. Private haulage maintains stables housing thousands of horses, one company stabling 2,000 horses at twenty depots strategically placed around the metropolis. Coal horses haul an average of thirty tons a week. Milkmen, the fire brigade, police, street cleaners, night-soil men all depend on the venerable breed.

When these horses grow too old or ill for haulage or slip and fall and are unable to rise again, even then are they useful.

Seven horse slaughtering depots in strategical locations round London are ever ready with clean carts to hasten, like fire engines, to the scene of a downed steed. Once delivered to the yard, the animal is slaughtered, skinned, and deboned in less than an hour. Skin and hooves go to the glue-maker. Bones to the button-maker. Tails and manes stuff sofas and are twisted into fishing-line. Hides are converted into carriage roofs and whips to lash other steeds. Boiled in huge copper kettles the meat is turned into food for London's prodigious population of cats and dogs. Even the shoes are recycled, sent to the farrier's to be welded and hammered to shod younger hooves and so back on the street within a matter of days.

The largest of these yards is in Wandsworth, South London. All that day, as London burned and the dead slaughtered the living and looters pillaged, slaughterhouse apprentices—the sons and nephews of the owners: the horse-knackering trade being mostly a family business—and a coterie of South London hooligans transported barrels of the new wine to a waiting barge. And as a glowering sunset joined the sporadic fires to paint a hellish skyline, a steam tug left Lambeth hauling the barge downriver.

Dirk Bogart tapped his shillelagh idly against his leg as he oversaw rival gang members—the Battersea Velvet Caps, the Wandsworth Scuttlers, some of his New Cut Boys and a contingent of Lambeth Lads: hooligans who, under normal circumstances would sooner trade blows than give the time of day—dump buckets of horses' blood into the river in an effort to lure the dead into following them.

And the floaters came.

In the gathering dark, the bodies looked like heaps of rags or squalid mounds of garbage. There was no stroke of arms, no flutter of feet churning the muckish water. They did not so much swim as preternaturally glide like some disgusting parody of merfolk as they drifted cross-current, defying the laws of nature. But then their very existence defied nature. Though he kept his mouth set in a grim frown, his gaze narrowed (it wouldn't do to let the lads see fear) Dirk's thick skin crawled at the sight.

The minister's boy, scrawny Lyle Trilling, his black-velvet cap immaculate while his arms were red to his rolled-up sleeves, shouted to him. "Do you think they'll board us?"

Impressively, the youngster appeared fearless, even excited, as if this was the greatest adventure of his young life. As it probably was. This would be a story that could buy a man a lifetime of drinks. If he lived to tell it.

"Patience, Trilling. Time for your bluster later. Back to work."

The last of the daylight was draining, but the city fires were lurid against the purpling sky. Bogart walked to the shoreward side of the barge, saw a floater surface not two dozen yards away and drift toward the craft. The blood was drawing them. They were less than an hour from their destination.

You might just get your wish, Trilling, he thought. *You just might.*

He turned and looked ahead at the steam tug hauling the barge. Squinting through the soot-filled smoke that belched from its tall black stack, he made out figures in the tug's stern. One of them, gangly Jeb

Wilkes, whom he trusted like a brother, waved. He'd made certain a couple of his lads were on the tug and some Elephant and Castle men were on the barge in case George Fish decided, if things got iffy, to cut the barge loose. He didn't trust the ascot-wearing, daisy-smelling son-of-a-bitch further than he could throw him. And though standing on the barge breathing in smoke and cinders was no worse than riding in a railway car with the windows open, it galled him to think of George Fish up there in the wheelhouse keeping his fuckin' ascot and bowler fresh. Thinking he'd like nothing better than to stave the dandy fucker's head in when this was over, he smacked the shillelagh against his leg.

***

From the tug's wheelhouse, George Fish watched the city burn. Flames licked from waterfront roofs, spread block to block, warehouse to warehouse, the smoke boiling up to meet the low-hanging clouds. Through the alternating ribbons of darkness and glare, the river cut a serpentine path. The scene was biblical, and with the dead rising from the water and swarming the dry land, apocalyptic.

"Hell of a sight," tug Captain Ernst Heppel observed.

The captain was as old as Methuselah—or at least looked it. With both hands on the oak wheel, feet planted on the varnished floor in a seaman's stance that rolled with the tide, his unkempt hair protruding from his soiled cap, and his grizzled chin curtain as grey and gnarled as the rope beard adorning the tug's bow, the man certainly struck an image of venerable antiquity.

George grunted agreement.

"This is what comes of man pursuing mammon and turning his back on God," the captain continued in a voice raspy from gin that nevertheless resonated with conviction and experience, as if he'd lived through famine and plague and knew a thing or two about calamity and human weakness. His watery blue eyes, set in the permanent squint of men who make their living on the water, twinkled, letting the younger man know he wasn't entirely serious.

"Behold," he said, "with a great plague will the Lord smite thy people, and thy children, and thy wives, and all thy goods and a catastrophe that could strike a city. The sword is without, and the pestilence and the famine within!"

"You should've been a preacher, old man," George said.

Heppel sneered. "And trade the river for a pulpit? Not to mention all the handshaking at the door!" He twisted his lips as if he were about to spit and raised his shoulders in a mock shudder. "Heaven forbid!"

The *Mary Belle*'s captain was certainly no bible-thumping, hymn-singing evangelist. His litanies tended to sea chanties, and none too pious at that.

Heppel pulled a short-stemmed pipe from his pocket and loaded it from a leather pouch. George inwardly groaned even before the old man struck a Lucifer and started puffing. The captain knew the river and George was grateful for his agreeing to haul them to Limehouse on the promise of generous pay at a later date, but his taste in tobacco was abominable. George, who purchased his special blend at Dellaport's near the

Elephant, was a connoisseur of the leaf and Heppel's was offensive.

"Do you have to smoke seaweed?"

"I reckon I'll smoke what I like. It's my tug, innit?"

Fish shrugged. "Have it your way, Gramps."

"And don't call me 'Gramps'! Sink me if you're kin of mine!"

"Just get us to Limehouse in time. If we don't get there by high water, this is for nothing."

Heppel's brows gathered like storm clouds over his watery eyes. "I've been sailing this river since your pappy was a gutter rat with shite running down his leg, so don't you go telling me about tides. We'll get there."

George hoped so. The water at Limehouse was level with the Thames only at high water. At low tide, the river was lower than the basin, and with the locks open, water would fall out of the basin into the river. For their plan to work, the locks had to be open and the dead had to be drawn into the basin.

He considered himself a rational man, certainly not one given to superstitious nonsense. He had a healthy respect for ghosts: he kept to his side of the street and they kept to theirs. But these river creatures were another matter. He'd seen violence, degradation, and the effects of poverty, but this was different. These things' existence was inexplicable: you couldn't blame their presence on poverty.

Was it as Heppel said? God's retribution for man's sin? A new type of plague visited on humankind? He hadn't thought much on God since his boyhood. Hadn't been inside a church in years. One thing he knew for certain though: If this was God's punishment for man's sin, the end times were upon them, because from what he'd observed of human nature, people didn't change and sin was the way of the world. For most people, sinning came more natural than praying.

A knock at the door interrupted his thoughts, and his Elephant and Castle mate, Ned Meadows, stuck his head in the wheelhouse.

"Georgie, the barge! It's been boarded!"

George stepped to the rear window. Below, men crowded the stern rail. Some yards off at the end of the tow line, a desperate struggle was taking place on the barge. From this distance in the darkness, it was difficult to tell the living from the dead, but he could just make out the knot of men holding off twice as many attackers.

As he watched, more floaters boarded, hauling themselves like lizards over the sides.

***

While the Thames barge lured floaters downriver in its bloody wake, a steam barge, hauling six lads and a dozen barrels of horse blood, did the same on the Regent's Canal. At 14-feet wide and 70 long, the narrowboat was the maximum length that would fit in the Regent's locks. Ornately painted blue and white with yellow trim, the canal boat was commonly used for hauling goods to and from the canal's many wharves, timber yards, sawmills, coal yards, furniture factories, gutta percha works and coach manufactories. Sometimes it carried casks of wine. Tonight, the claret, still warm from the knacker's yard, was of a very different vintage. The hot tang of horses' blood hung in the air as two muscular lads ladled it out over the gunnels by the bucketsful while three others stood ready with long poles to ward off any floater that might try to board. They'd have to be quick as the dead were surprisingly fast and liable to pop up anywhere.

Quincy Bird, leader of the City Road Gang, manned the stern, the thick beam of the extended tiller in his hand as he gazed over the small cabin that housed the steam engine and guided the boat between the banks as it chugged past warehouses and lumberyards and sawmills and ironworks and gasworks and factories followed by stretches of brick houses followed by more industries around bends and under bridges and railway trestles, cutting a torturous path through the heart of London.

The streets on either side of the canal were dark and eerily silent, the backs of the homes, factories and warehouses they passed shuttered and deserted. Terror of what dwelt in the city's waterways had driven the populace further inland. The lamplighters had abandoned their duty. South beyond the gasworks and factories and houses, the city was burning. Though they couldn't see the fires raging in the heart of the city and along the Thames, the rising columns of smoke and the lowering clouds glowed with a ruddy light.

They'd been lucky so far. Setting out from St. Pancras Basin, they'd avoided having to go farther upstream into affluent Kentish Town where they'd likely be shot for brigands. Most of the attacks reported came from downstream anyway, especially below Acton's Lock from Victoria Park to Limehouse. Starting farther down the canal also gave them the advantage of having fewer locks to navigate. The locks were the most dangerous part of their task in luring the bogles to Limehouse Basin. The Regent's Canal fell over a thousand feet from Camden Town to Limehouse

Basin, requiring them to stop at each lock, where someone had to get out and open the paddles by fitting the L-shaped windlass into the locking mechanism and cranking the paddles up allowing canal water to fill the lock. When the water level equalized, your shore crew muscled the gate open by pushing the balance beam, you steered in, your lock crew closed the gate and paddle behind you, then opened the paddle and gate at the far end. It was proper etiquette observed by all that upon exiting the lock, you closed the paddle and gate. But that consumed time in which you were vulnerable to attack. Tonight, they were leaving all gates open to increase the water flow down to the basin.

Quincy set his not inconsiderable jaw and scowled past the stack that rose from the flat roof belching smoke and cinders in their wake. It wouldn't do to let the boys see the worry that gnawed his liver.

Stripped down to his undershirt, blond, broad-shouldered, muscular Dewey Haines looked like a Viking as he tirelessly heaved buckets of blood over the gunnel. The lad never seemed to get cold. Even in winter he could be seen hatless with his jacket open as he took long strides down the frozen street. On the starboard side, Patsy Kennedy of the Dove Row squids, as swarthy as Dewey was pale and as ugly as a bulldog's ass, a head shorter than Dewey and four stone lighter, dipped his bucket and flung its contents overboard with as much determination and vigor as the bigger man. Quincy's own City Road compatriot, Roger Ascombe, was hard at work removing barrel heads. You can't dip a bucket in a bung hole, so Roger was removing head and quarter hoops with a cooper's hammer and hoop driver. It would be faster to smash in the heads with a hatchet, but barrels were worth a pretty penny and he and Roger figured to reassemble and sell them when this was over. Dove Row's Jimmy Dawes and Haines' Golden Lane mate, skinny albino Newt Whipple, kept watch on either side, ready with long poles that doubled as quarterstaffs to push off any floater that tried to board.

They were all from North London and normally any meeting ended in blows. Old rivalries, matters of territory and pride, like traditions, had to be kept up. So it was amazing to see them working side by side— in unison as if they were members of the same gang and had drilled at this for weeks.

No doubt when this was over, they'd be back at each other's throats—he looked forward to the day, in fact—but for now, they had to cooperate.

"Coming up to the tunnel," Roger called. The wiry greyhound of a youth didn't sound happy about the prospect.

And there it was. At the sight of the black maw beneath the brick arch, Quincy suppressed a shudder. The Angel Tunnel ran 960 yards beneath the streets and houses of Islington. Nine hundred sixty yards of claustrophobic blackness and no light save the boat's single lantern.

"Steady boys," he called, forcing his voice to keep low and calm as worry bit deeper into his liver.

Dewey and Patsy put down their buckets. Jimmy Dawes and Newt Whipple readied their poles to push against the tunnel walls should Quincy veer to either side.

As they slipped into darkness.

6

WHILE QUINCY AND HIS crew offloaded their cargo of blood, Kate and more than a dozen girls from rival gangs worked their way up the canal opening locks. The idea was to open all the locks from St. Pancras to Limehouse. If both were successful and they met up somewhere along the system, they could abandon the canal while the increased flood flushed the floaters down to the basin where Will and the others would, with the help of whatever gods there be, destroy them.

So far, they'd been lucky. The Commercial Road Lock at the mouth of the canal where it poured into the basin was open, as were the Solomon Lane Lock and Johnson's Locke above. They met slight resistance at Solomon Lane, shoving two floaters into the lock until the lower gates were open. The surge of falling water swept the creatures downstream.

Seldom more than seven feet wide, the towpath wound along one side of the dark waterway. A long wall of leaning board fences separated the cindered yards of tenements on their right. On the opposite side loomed the hulks of wharves and warehouses. Ahead, the canal narrowed where it passed under Gunmakers Arms Bridge. Leaning telegraph poles rose out of the

53

gloom on Bridge Street above. With London afire and its citizens fleeing, the lamplighters had given up on lighting its streets. However, the darkness was not absolute; even from three miles away, the fires in central London, reflecting off the underbellies of the lowering clouds, illuminated the path in shifting garish light.

They were nearing the Mile End Lock when the attack came.

All of them, even Queen Jane, were dressed for business—to wit, they wore the common working-class male attire of 'costers, vanboys and 'prentices: waistcoats, corduroy trousers and hobnailed boots. Dirty Deidre of the notoriously violent Wandsworth Scuttlers and her lumbering, sour-faced cohort, Mags Goody, brandished the added lethalness of rib-smashing steel toe caps on their boots. Razor Lil, obviously rethinking the practicality of using her trademark straight razor on the undead, and her girls, Maud and Pru, hefted railway spike mauls, their ash hafts shortened to make two-handed "wood chopping" swings more practical at close quarters.

With so many simmering grudges and unsettled accounts, Kate expected some quarreling but, despite the need for silence, bickering had plagued their journey from the start, Dirty Deidre being the chief offender. The big woman clanked her steel-tipped boots down inches from Midge Tibbet's heels, not making an effort to keep quiet but breathing down the Limehouse Reaper's neck even as she kept up a running banter.

"Tibbet here's got eyes for yer Small Tom," Deidre said to her gang mate. Though Mags walked beside her, Deirdre raised her voice for the group's benefit. "Whaddaya think of that Mags?"

True to his name, Small Tom stood no higher than Mags' breasts, his diminutive size useful for fanlight-jumping. Regularly seen hanging around Mags like an inadequate shadow, the wiry burglar doted on the bigger woman. Make no mistake, for crib-cracking a tall girl and a petite fellow were every bit the equal, or even superior, of any two regular guys. In addition to which Tom was an excellent featherweight, proficient with the gloves in the square ring and even more adept at head-butting and jaw-cracking in the raw. With Mags for muscle and Small Tom for window-entering, the couple made a profitable pair.

"Does she now?" Mags growled, equally loud.

Deidre, still riding the rush of shoving a floater into the canal, was naturally wild and made wilder by her appetite for cocaine. Her eyes were round, her face twisted with a savage grin as she baited the female Reaper. "She does indeed!"

Kate knew what Deidre was doing. As the Scuttlers hailed from South London, miles from the Reapers' East London home, Deidre's taunting wasn't about territory but with establishing bull goose rights. While not the most dominant North London gang, the Reapers were certainly well-known for the violence of their attacks, often employing railway spikes tied to chains instead of belts in their skirmishes. Even now said spikes dangled from chains as the Reapers strode ahead of the Scuttlers. So far, Midge was showing surprising restraint.

"You got eyes for my Tom?" Mags poked Midge in the back.

"I'll thank'e to keep yer bleedin' paws to yerself, ya lumberin' golem!" Midge hissed and let out a length of chain, dropping the railway spike dangling at her side a foot in preparation for battle. The edge to her voice sent a chill up Kate's spine.

City Road's Winnie Tuttle sniggered. Deidre silenced her with a withering glance.

"Why don't you both shut yer gobs before you draw the whole canal down on us!" Peg Dyer said, equally loud.

"Who're you talking to?" Mags' fingers curled into fists. Mags might be dimwitted, but she was brutal.

Kate's grip tightened on the five-foot-long railway pry bar she carried. This prattling had to stop. They had work to do and no time to draw unwanted attention. She was about to shush them all when she saw it was too late.

From the murk beneath the bridge, a hulking silhouette stepped into the path.

And behind it another. And another.

Bloated disfigured monstrosities that took on hideous features as they stepped into the garish light.

Kate froze, as did the girls around her, not from fear—though cold sluiced through her veins raising goosebumps and chilling her bones—but to assess the enemy.

How many? she wondered, squinting into the underpass, trying to make out the shapes emerging behind the first three.

"Maybe we should go back." Forty Elephants' Claire Alden voiced the general feeling.

"We can't," Dove Row's Annie Dawes said. "We have to open the lower locks for the plan to work."

"We could go around them. Use the streets," Lambeth's Ruby Morton said beside Kate.

"We can't." New Cut's Arlene Myers was looking behind them.

Kate followed her gaze.

They'd been making so much noise they hadn't heard the tread of wet footfalls on the cinder path or seen the shambling shapes blocking their retreat.

Cut off. Nowhere to run. Ahead, behind, equally dangerous.

In that frozen moment, a wet arm slapped over the edge of the towpath and, streaming water, a bedraggled head and shoulders rose from the canal.

***

The Regent's Canal Dock connected the Regent's Canal with the River Thames at Limehouse. Originally the basin between the canal and river was small with an island in the middle where canal craft could tie up to await the tide before passing through the lock and so shuttle cargo back and forth between sea-going ships and canal barges. Eventually, grander ideas and Parliamentary funding prevailed and a basin large enough to admit sea-going vessels was constructed. Steam colliers could now enter the basin, transfer their coal to lighters for onward transit to the new canal-side gas works, and timber from the Baltics and North and South America could be off-loaded onto timber yards to be transported to Shoreditch furniture makers.

Two locks connected the basin with the river: a larger one for colliers and sailing ships and a smaller one for lighters and other small craft. The Ship Lock with its swing bridge was too large for their purposes, so Will and his crew concentrated on the smaller barge lock. It would be touch and go and much depended on George Fish and Dirk Bogart's arrival coinciding with high water.

From his vantage standing on the Narrow Street swing bridge over the Ship Lock, Will could look out onto the deserted River Thames and at the activity behind him in the Limehouse Basin. Beside him, Police Constable Foley held a spyglass to his eye. While it was dark out on the river where the only signs of activity were bats darting near the shore, the dock was lit by glaring arc lamps mounted on eighty-foot-tall posts spaced along the middle of the quays. The garish light illuminated the wharves and decks of ships with a light brighter than the full moon and while Foley's back was washed in its colorless radiance, his front remained in shadow.

"Any sign?" Will asked.

Foley lowered the spyglass, shook his head. "Not yet. We've got time."

Foley was referring to the tide: the river outside the bottom lock gate was still lower than the basin above.

The boiling clouds in the west glowed a deep, malignant red, as if the fire had spread to the sky. Columns of black smoke rose in the distance over the roofs and chimneys of warehouses and offices. The city was burning, its citizenry fleeing. Will wondered how much would be left after tonight. Would life ever be the same after this epidemic? And if they failed . . .

Will squinted back at the warehouses and granaries and timber yards that surrounded the basin. A forest of masts rose over the Regent Canal jetties. Below the great sailing ships, smaller lighters and barges clustered like terriers around stallions. Unlike the river, the dock was anything but silent. The shouts of men readying for the assault vied with the steady pounding from the engine house that powered the hydraulic cranes on the north-west and south-west quays. The cranes were used for unloading and loading coal and oil barrels. One wharf housed thirty-five free-standing tanks for oil and turpentine of various capacities up to 100 tons each. The tanks were filled by hydraulic pumps from a corrugated-iron shed containing sump-tanks fed by troughs into which barrels, unloaded from barges by crane, were emptied. A similar shed, containing three 1,500-gallon and two 450-gallon tanks, was used for barrel-filling. Will was pleased to see the makeshift system of pipes redirecting the oil into the basin was nearing completion.

Several stevedores and a number of sailors remained at the dock when Will and his crew arrived. When they learned of the cargo Fish and Bogart were bringing, many high-tailed it out of the basin; some stayed to help. Will was grateful for the assistance. The men would be needed. They knew how to operate the dock's equipment and where supplies were stored. And the two professional crane operators were a godsend.

"Will."

Working over in his mind the sequence of what had to happen to destroy the floaters, Will was so engrossed he hadn't noticed Chauncey Bellows approach. Despite his broken wrist which was done up very prettily in a linen sling, Chauncey had insisted on helping. As there was nothing wrong with his legs, Will had assigned him as runner.

"Chaunce?"

"Stoat asked for you to come down to the freezer."

***

The tunnel was a half-circle of hell.

On an average day—or even night—it was an annoyance. There was no towpath and for those engineless crafts that, even in these modern times, were towed by horse, a crew member had to lead the beast through the streets and meet you at the mooring on the other side. But even if you had a steam engine and a dozen lanterns, the passage seemed endless and you felt the weight of the city crushing down . . . until you were back out into the open air and you could breathe again.

Sometimes it was even fun—when you had a little grog in you and, running through the tunnel, you and your mates tried to outdo each other shouting vulgarities or you belted a bawdy ballad at the top of your lungs and the close walls amplified and redoubled your voice as echoes bounced off the bricks.

But tonight, it wasn't just the dark or the long half-circle stretching to a vanishing point with no end of the tunnel in sight or the ponderous sense of roads and houses and factories and churches ready to break through the arch just above your head. There was the subliminal terror of being in the dark with an unutterable horror that bit and tore but left its victims neither dead nor alive.

The slow chug of the engine echoed off the moist bricks. The sound of the lads tapping their staffs against the walls making minor adjustments to save him from oversteering was amplified till it sounded like some peg-legged sailor stumping his way along a wharf. Everyone's ears were cocked for the slightest sound. Anything that was out of place, that didn't belong, that told them they were not alone.

It happened in the blink of an eye. They were halfway through when something yanked Jimmy Dawe's pole and he pitched overboard. Quincy heard a loud *smack* that must have been Dawe's head cracking against the brick wall followed by a splash. Then nothing.

Absolutely nothing.

There was a stunned moment when Roger and Newt Whipple raised their poles to strike in case something tried to board, all of them frantically scanning the water for a sign of Dawes, as Quincy eased off the throttle, torn between searching for the Dove Row boy and making a run for it.

Nothing but the quiet chug of the idling engine and the plash of water lapping against their hull.

Quincy laid on the throttle and got them through the tunnel.

7

THEY WERE PASSING UNDER the grim visage of the Tower of London when the floaters boarded.

With Dirk supervising and the rest of the men working at the barge's stern, no one realized they'd been boarded till Dirk turned to see who was shouting. Jeb and a few others stood at the tug's stern-rail waving and yelling, but he didn't need their help to see what they were pointing at. Three floaters had somehow hauled themselves onto the barge and were making their way aft.

So, the fuckers can climb!

He filed the information away along with other useful tidbits like beware coppers wearing vulcanized rubber soles and rainy nights are best for breaking into warehouses.

"Head's up, men!" he shouted. But a quick glance told him they'd seen their company. In a matter of seconds, they'd dropped their buckets, wiped bloody hands on their trousers, grabbed their weapons—knives, axe handles, a pickaxe and a couple of iron pry bars—and gathered for battle. Smacking the shillelagh against his palm, and with a wild grin on his face, Dirk started toward the floaters.

"Hey!"

Dirk turned at the shout. It was Lyle Trilling. He'd got his wish. A floater was half over the rear gunnel. Trilling cracked its skull with his axe handle and the creature slid back into the water.

Dirk pointed to four men: "You come with me." And to three others: "You boys help Trilling.

By the time they reached the bow, two more floaters had joined the first and more were coming over the sides.

***

Will shivered as he stepped through the inner door of the airlock. The freezer was a refrigerating plant. Stored in its larders, stacked floor to ceiling, were 300 tons of New Zealand sheep carcasses. Normally the hoofless, headless, gutted and skinned carcasses would be hard as stone and white with frost, but the boys had built a fire in the center of the room and the carcasses were thawing. Blood and water ran down the stacks and spread across the floor. Melting ice dripped from the ceiling.

The local Millwallers, Jimmy Stoat and Nate Dunham, stood beside him. Snowflakes drifting from the ceiling glittered in the beam of Jimmy's bull's eye lantern.

Nearly a third of the carcasses had been sped along roller conveyors out the door to the basin's edge where other Millwallers sent them splashing into the basin. On his way in, Will had seen this end of the pool glutted with sheep carcasses bobbing in the water.

"They're not thawing fast enough," Will said.

"They'll thaw in the water," Nate said.

It was true enough; the water was warm. Will wrinkled his nose. The blood reek was sharp. If they could draw the floaters into the basin, the carcasses would keep them in the water. In theory at least.

Unless they only drank human blood.

***

The passage through the City Road Lock was tense but uneventful.

Luck was with them: the lock was full. Patsy Kennedy got out and opened the gate with the lock key while Dewey and Newt stood guard with their staves and Roger looped a rope around a mooring post but didn't tie it in case they had to cast off in a hurry. Quincy kept the engine idling while Patsy closed the gate and raced to the far end where he fitted the windlass on the spindle and cranked the lower gate paddles. When the water reached equilibrium, he swung the gates open and Quincy steered out. The crew jumped aboard and they were off. The whole affair was over in a matter of nerve-wracking minutes.

But as they approached Sturt's Lock, they saw they would not be so lucky.

Three deaders hung about, two on the side housing the lock mechanism, one on the other. They appeared to be watching their approach, as if they'd heard the chug of the engine or seen their lantern.

"Whadda we do?" Newt said.

Though the Golden Laner was skinny as an itinerant preacher and pale as an onion, Quincy had seen him swing a chain in a skirmish and knew he was no slacker. Nervous was all. He was feeling a bit skittish himself.

"We take them," he said.

"You sure?" Patsy said. "After what happened to Jimmy . . ."

Quincy understood. Patsy was going to have to deliver the news to Jimmy's mom. Funny, he'd never thought of other gang members having moms. (Or sisters—that's right, Jimmy has a sister that'd have to be told as well.) Only as rivals for territories and resources.

"We go in," he repeated.

Patsy started to say something, frowned, nodded.

Quincy backed the throttle to an idle as they approached. "Dewey, Patsy, you guys take those two." He inclined his head toward the ghoulish creatures swaying on the lock side. "Newt, you take out the other one."

"And leave you and Roger on the boat?" Newt said, his thin lips a sneer: Roger was Quincy's brother-in-arms. "What's to keep you from leaving us behind?"

Quincy just glared at him. Newt was the first to look down. "Yeah, okay," he said, his Adam's apple bobbing as he nodded.

***

They chose to go forward.

The odds ahead and behind being equal, continuing up-canal had the advantage of furthering their mission. Retreat translated into failure.

Statuesque, yellow-haired Mary Haines said, "My brother's up there somewhere, risking his life. We can't do less. I'm going on." The Golden Laner hefted her hatchet.

"Mine too," Dove Row's little Annie Dawes added, and to everyone's surprise started forward on her own. That cinched it. No one cared to be seen as cowardly or to let a rival gang do her one better.

Deidre and Mags fisted their foot-long knives and,

raising a war cry that rendered moot any further attempt at stealth, started to push past Midge Tibbets and Peg Dyer, but not to be outdone the Limehouse Reapers rushed ahead swinging their spiked chains.

Kate found herself in the middle of the surging crowd, too close to swing her pry bar properly. Then the troops closed, and the stench of black water and rotten flesh seared her nostrils as bloated hands big as balloons grasped arms and hair, and teeth sank into living flesh, and she found herself jabbing the pointed end of the iron into pocked, noseless faces and more than one scream told her that some of her party would not be returning home that night.

At least not as they had started out.

8

SOON AS THE PROW of the barge grazed the bulkhead, Patsy and Dewey leapt out and ran in swinging their poles like Little John crossing staves with Robin Hood. Dewey landed a terrific blow to one floater's head, literally caving in the creature's skull with a sickening crunch and hurling the thing into the water. Patsy wasn't so lucky. He, too, swung, but his target, seemingly unhampered by its sopping jacket and trousers, was quick and caught the pole inches from its head, wrenched it out of Patsy's hands and flung it over his shoulder. The thing was on Patsy in an instant. Taller than the Dove Rower, it bent over him as it bore him to his knees. Brown teeth snapped at him as he fended it off. The river reek of it burned his nose. Then it was lifted off him as Dewey's staff caught it in the throat and flung it backwards. For a moment he thought he was going into the drink as his assailant clung to him, taking him with it, but a second blow from Dewey's pole knocked it to the stone platform, and before it could rise, the Golden Laner stood over it and rammed the end of the staff into its eye. The ash wood punched through the socket and lodged deep in its skull. The thing spasmed, then lay still.

"You killed it," Patsy said, rising.

"Looks like," Dewey said.

On the other side of the lock, Newt Whipple wasn't faring well. Obese from the bloat of corruption, the female floater had him on the ground, bared teeth snapping at him, dripping hair nearly obscuring the youngster's face. Pressing his staff under its throat, Newt struggled to fend off his attacker. But even as Patsy looked for a way to get across the lock, Roger rushed onto the dock carrying a bucket which he used to slam the deader off Newt and then pounded the thing's head with the bucket till its skull was a mass of bone and brain and its limbs stopped thrashing and it lay as still as its partner.

Without hesitating an instant longer, Patsy yanked the windlass from his belt, fitted it to the lock mechanism and cranked as if his life depended on it. Within moments the canal boat was sliding into the lock and he was winching the paddles closed and hurrying to the far end to open the lower gate. Dewey didn't wait for the water to completely equalize; when it looked close enough, he forced the gate open and the steamer slid out with the spill of water.

Before Patsy turned to race back and reopen the upper gate, he saw the floater Dewey knocked into the water spiraling downstream on the surge.

***

They were outnumbered.

Stabbing didn't slow them. Even punching an iron pry bar through their chests and out their backs didn't stop them. As Sandy Sykes learned the hard way. No filing that useful tidbit away for later for him. When he slammed his iron through an attacker, the creature kept coming, running itself down the bar and battening on Sykes and shaking its head like a dog tearing off a long strip of the Elephant and Castle member's face. Bashing their skulls in seemed to be the only way to immobilize them. Turned out, Dirk Bogart's shillelagh was the perfect tool for the job. One good crack to the top or side of the skull and the creatures fell, meat and bone driven deep into their rotten brains.

But the bastards kept coming.

Resting his dripping shillelagh to catch his breath, Dirk spared a glance at the tug. The men clustered in its stern watched, helpless to aid their fellows on the barge. With its higher hull, the tug seemed safe enough.

Dirk caught a floater under the chin, spraying bone and teeth and fetid water-sodden flesh. He ducked a grasping hand, came up beside his attacker and brought the shillelagh down in an overhand blow, driving the weapon's bulbous end into its skull. Another monster toppled. The deck was crowded with corpses, human and otherwise, and slippery with the spilled viscera of monster and man.

And still the deaders came, swarming over the gunnels, taking down men who continued to fight even as teeth and nails ripped them apart. Two survivors, having abandoned the stern, were battling their way forward. Some of the dead pursued, others licked blood from the deck or dunked their heads into open barrels as if bobbing for apples.

Dirk glimpsed Lyle Trilling coming forward. The floaters didn't attack him, and from the way the boy lurched and grasped with one hand while the other arm hung at his side, he could see the youngster had joined them.

*****

What was left of the party fled up the towpath. Three of their ranks had fallen—Bess Jessup and Connie Willis—and Kate had seen Fay Allen—one of her own, a girl she had grown up with jumping rope and playing Hopscotch and holding the older pickpockets' swag while they pursued further plunder—go down not more than a yard in front of her, borne to the path by three of the living dead, had seen her nose and cheek ripped free by a savage jerk of one eyeless horror's teeth while another popped the buttons of her waistcoat and burrowed its muzzle in her guts. Kate's brain throbbed with the kaleidoscope of bloody images.

Plump, sarcastic Nell Quigley was bleeding out from the gaping wound in her thigh, her eyes alternately rolling back as her head lolled upon her shoulder and starting awake in wide-eyed terror as she stumbled on supported by Annie Dawes and City Road's Babs Nye. But for how long? Already the toes of her boots furrowed the cinders as the girls hauling her in the group's wake fell farther back. And was it true? Did the fallen rise as one of *them*?

To say the battle had been a nightmare was an understatement. Nothing Kate ever dreamt matched the mind-shattering horror of what she'd experienced. No fight against rival gang compared. As a girl—before she became immured to such sights—she'd seen a dog crushed beneath a wagon wheel, its guts burst upon the cobbles. She'd puked and for weeks the image pursued her into dreamland. Not even her uncle's tales of the Indian Uprising and what he'd witnessed at Cawnpore—a well gorged with the dismembered bodies of British women and children, piles of bloody children's clothing in a courtyard, a tree trunk smeared with children's brains, severed women's hair blowing in the wind where it had been caught in tree branches—compared with the visceral horror of witnessing first-hand the slaughter of people she knew by preternatural killers.

Shuddering, she wiped her face with her sleeve, still feeling the slime of wet decayed flesh. A scratch where a floater's nail had dug into her cheek stung.

The leaning hulk of a steam sawmill rose up beside them. Its thundering engines were silent for once, its towering soot-blackened chimneys smokeless. The rail yards across the canal were likewise deserted, eerily void of industry. It was quiet enough to hear the sound of flowing water and . . .

Footsteps!

A band of men poured out of a lane onto the towpath, cutting them off. Like Kate and the girls, they wore waistcoats and cords that had seen better days and flat caps or bowlers above their unwashed faces. There was perhaps a score of them. The girls were outnumbered.

"What've we here?" crowed a beetle-browed, bullet-headed brute.

"Why, they're girls!" another said, marveling at the discovery.

"Lou's right," said a third, a skinny, pock-faced thug with bad teeth and the face of a weasel.

"Looks like they're going to a party," observed a fourth, eyeing the assortment of weapons the girls carried. The men were mostly armed with sticks, though some hefted pry bars, convenient for entering houses now that the citizenry was fleeing and the law distracted.

Marauders, Kate thought. Seizing an opportunity. She couldn't fault them. Most of the gangs would be doing the same if they weren't engaged in saving the city.

"Let us pass," Kate snarled, baring her teeth and lifting her iron.

Several of the ruffians laughed. The first brute spat a stream of tobacco juice across the path into the canal.

"You heard her," Razor Lil said, stepping up beside Kate. The high-cheekboned Drury Laner rested her spike maul on her shoulder as casually as if she were a rail worker taking a breather.

Midge and Peg stepped forward, rail spikes swinging at the end of their chains. Mary Haines cracked her knuckles, her grim smile worthy of a Valkyrie or a Berserker. Deidre grinned like the blood-hungry demon she was.

Some of the brigands looked worried, but the leaders merely grinned as if they looked forward to the encounter.

Weasel-face made a half-circle around the Bow Commoner twins, Fanny and Alice Dupree, two dirty-blondes with narrow faces but fine figures. "Twins!" he crooned. "Dibs!"

Mags Goody made the first move. She took two steps forward and raised her knife as if about to stab someone. It was a fake, as Bullet-head learned when her steel-capped boot connected with his balls. He dropped his pry bar and doubled over.

Then Peg and Midge and Deidre and Beth and Lil and Kate and the others were among the men, kicking and flailing and laying iron to skulls. After coming this far and suffering losses, they weren't about to be raped by these unwashed sewer rats.

One of the men had a barker. Kate saw Weasel-face raise the revolver. Looking down its bore at point-blank range was as chilling as a plunge into ice water. The bulldog barked. Kate felt a hot wind an inch from her ear. Then Weasel-face was backing away, as were several of the marauders and some of the girls. Risking a glance over her shoulder, Kate saw why.

Floaters!

A dozen or more of the dead, likely drawn by the noise, had joined the melee. Already one of the girls was down—Kate couldn't see who, so tight was the press—and two of the men. Kate and New Cut Beth must have had the same thought for they exchanged a nod and, turning, drove a wedge through the milling brigands. The rest of the girls followed, closing ranks, no longer bickering amongst themselves but united against a common enemy. Whether they knew their history or not, their maneuver was like a Roman phalanx arrowing through a disorderly Celtic charge.

In moments they were clear, leaving their would-be rapists to battle the dead.

They didn't look back.

***

Newt hadn't escaped entirely whole. Propped against the engine house, his long legs splayed on the deck, the lad was groaning. His pale flesh had darkened and sweat poured down his thin face, soaked his shirt.

His right hand was missing two fingers.

Dewey had donated his shirt for a bandage, but any further medical attention would have to wait.

From where he stood behind the engine house manning the tiller, Quincy couldn't see Newt, but he could hear him groan. The boy was in terrific pain. More pain than the severed fingers should have caused—though that would be pain enough for weaker men—men who had wobblers and coffee served at their breakfast table while they pored over the morning paper's financial news. But Newt was of tougher stock, as were all the rag-tag hooligans that came up on the street never knowing when their next meal would come until they learned the skills that would put food in their mouths and ready in their pockets. And to hell with John Law and the man who had wobblers and coffee with his morning news.

Quincy spared a moment of concentration to watch the men working in the foredeck. Dewey and Patsy emptied their buckets over the sides as fast as they could fill them while Roger, no longer muscling the tops off the barrels, removing hoops with hammer and driver so they could later sell them, was busy hatcheting the lids of those remaining.

Quincy tried his best to keep his eye on the twists and turns of the canal ahead as he sped past darkened streets and houses—long and narrow, canal boats pivoted on their middles, so it was all too easy to oversteer and put the bow into a bulkhead—but images of dead eyes staring at them from the lock landing and the smack of Jimmy's skull striking bricks and the splash of his body hitting the water . . . and the thought of what lay beneath those waters . . . filled him with a cold he'd never felt. Not the cold that bit into your bones when curbside water froze and the wind howled out of the north and cut through your too-thin coat, but the cold hand of dread. It was one thing to deal with rivals or coppers or hunger, but this!

He grit his teeth and shook himself. *Snap out of it. Get a grip.*

How many more locks to go? Five? Six? He knew the answer, knew the route by heart, but his mind was abuzz, his senses heightened to a silent scream. How was the crew coming up the canal faring? Would they meet and celebrate their victory by abandoning the canal for safer streets? Or would their efforts be in vain?

Patsy and Dewey dipped and dumped. Roger's hatchet rose and fell. And still Newt groaned.

Was that all it took? A bite and you were one of them? Then they were damned. All the more important they complete their mission, draw the floaters down to the basin where, hopefully, Will Tagget and Bill Drummond and that fucking slop Foley could finish them.

A thump shook the barge. He tightened his grip on the tiller as the craft jittered on its central axis. He backed off the throttle till he got her straightened.

"What was that?" Patsy shouted.

"Dunno," he said, sweeping his gaze over the dark water.

He saw them the same time Dewey called out.

"Floaters!"

"I see them."

They slipped through the water like fantastic visions of darkest nightmare. Like demonic merfolk, dressed in sodden clothing that should have borne them to the depths but didn't, they came on from either side, not stroking the water or scissoring their legs as swimmers do, nor paddling like otters nor flippering like dolphins, but gliding cross-current, unhampered by the canal's flow. What he was seeing was impossible, but then so was the presence of these creatures that had once been among the high and low of London society, who had once walked the streets of the Great Leviathan and eaten their eel pies and bangers and toast and wobblers and washed them down with coffee or beer, who cut deals on the floor of the London Exchange or over a wheelbarrow of fish in Billingsgate, who, come Sundays, sat in pulpits listening to the minister drone or stayed abed late sleeping off Saturday's gin. What couldn't possibly be, was. The very reality of what he was seeing was apocalyptic. How often had he passed street-corner Elijahs preaching the end times and not given a moment's thought to their message? His guts roiled at the thought that—whatever they accomplished tonight—the world was doomed.

But as unnerving as the sight was and though the hair on his head rippled with preternatural fear as he watched the oily smears grease through the black water, it also strengthened his resolve to drive on instead of running the boat to shore and fleeing into the streets.

Newt's groan carried over the water. The swimmers glided closer. The barge chugged toward the unknown.

9

ILL DRUMMOND AND THE little Bow Commoner Alby Budge came up the walk to the swing bridge where Will and Police Constable Foley were anxiously watching for Fish and Bogart's arrival and arguing what to do if the tug didn't make it or arrived after high water or if the living dead would even enter the lock. Both remembered how the severed hand, in trying to escape, adapted to its environment. Did the floaters have some sort of primitive survival instinct that would keep them from entering the basin? Foley suggested they might march their troops back toward town and help the authorities destroy them. But only halfheartedly. They might be of some small service, but the floaters would still infest the waterways. And there was still the chance Quincy Bird's crew and Kate and the girls would succeed in flushing the canal's floaters down to the basin.

Thinking of Kate brought a lump to his throat. She could handle herself, and she had some tough company with her, but still . . . He'd be glad when this was over and he could put his arms around her and feel her hair against his cheek and smell her perfume. He made a mental note to lift her something nice the next time he was in the Walk.

Drummond was wiping his fingers on a handkerchief that had once been red. Now it was as black as his hands. His face, looking cadaverous in the glaring arc light, was streaked with fuel oil and his waistcoat and trousers were ruined. If anything, Budge was even filthier, looking as if he'd actually fallen in a pool of oil.

"Pipeline's complete," Drummond announced when he came within hearing. The relentless pounding from the great piston in the octagonal hydraulic accumulator tower that powered the capstans, lock gates, swing bridge and cranes made talking difficult.

Will turned the spyglass on the Regent's Canal Dock. Though the river was a darkling plane filled with galleons of ghostly mist, the ten-acre dock with its basin and ships, quays, machinery, storehouses and sheds was starkly illuminated under the harsh arc lights.

Sure enough, a maze of cast-iron pipe ran from the sheds containing the giant oil tanks to the water's edge.

"Pumps hooked up?" Foley asked.

"Yep," Drummond replied. Budge's head bobbed.

"Have you tested them?"

Drummond frowned at the constable, as if he'd been insulted. "Whadda you think, copper?"

"Just asking." Foley was taller than the Drury Lane boy, his gaze more domineering. Neither lowered his eyes.

Ignoring them, Will panned the spyglass across the dock. The Millwallers had done yeomen's service hauling the thawing sheep into the basin. The carcasses had drifted and now were everywhere, bobbing like grotesque melting ice blocks. Blood slicked the dark water. Lads stood about armed and ready. Scanning their weapons, he saw railway pry bars, digging bars, crowbars, wrecking bars, railway spike mauls, pickaxes. One big Clerkenwell boy wielded a sledgehammer one-handed as if it were a mallet. He saw a few firearms—grandfather's squirrel guns, a couple breech-loaders brought back by India campaigners, a couple Webleys, but no repeating rifles. Two boys had found some casks of gunpowder in one of the ship's holds. No one had come up with a plan for how or where to use them. He hoped they didn't blow themselves up.

Despite the assembled troops hailing from rival gangs, his heart lifted at the sight. They may not make the pages of the *Illustrated Police News*, but the image would forever be etched in his memory. They might not have the crimson tunics of dragoons or the blue of sailors, but any floater that attempted to haul itself onto the dock would get what for.

A few sailors milled about on ships, the rest had pitched in. They'd all been warned the plan was to burn the floaters in the water, which meant the loss of ships. Two of the three-masters had made it out the Ship Lock. The rest didn't have enough crew to manage. Will thought about that. Ships—perhaps even the Regent's Canal Dock itself with its coal bunkers, timber yards and oil tanks—would go up in flames. The city would not thank them for their efforts, rather the ship owners, the oil, coal and timber companies, and magistrates would howl for their blood.

As if reading his mind, Foley said to Budge, "You know we'll probably all go to prison after tonight."

"Newgate, you think?" Budge said, his brows knit with concern.

Foley huffed at the notion of a debtor's prison. "Nothing so gentile for the likes of us. The Wandsworth whipping post's more likely."

Budge blanched at the thought of the notorious prison where inmates could be whipped to within an inch of their lives for the smallest infraction. Keeping his smile to himself, Will played along. "If we're lucky. I wouldn't rule out hanging. London thrives on trade. Destroying the shareholders' source of revenue is the same as treason. And you know what they do to traitors?"

Budge swallowed hard and passed a hand over his throat, further blackening his flesh. The scaffold obviously very much on his mind.

"But it won't come to that," Will said. "We'll hoof it when we're finished here and pick up some swag on our way home." The latter he delivered behind his cupped hand as if to share the news only with Budge but speaking loud enough for Foley and Drummond to hear over the chug of the generator.

Budge grinned, relieved at the alternative ending to his life's brief story.

"Good job," Will said to Drummond, nodding toward the dock.

Lifting the spyglass, he returned his attention to the river.

If only Fish would get here, he thought but saw no sign of tug or barge.

***

They'd attracted a crowd.

The floaters drifted alongside now, not attempting to board, not getting in their way but leaving the lane before them open. At four miles an hour, the canal boat passed their entourage, but there were always more, drifting alongside, as if they knew the lock lay ahead and the living would have to stop and deal with the dead.

A gasworks swept by on the right, cylindrical holders looming against a glowering sky. The Haggerston Bridge came into view. Acton Lock was minutes away.

"Rog, those barrels open?" Quincy called to his City Road mate.

"They're open."

"Dump them."

"All of them?" Patsy called.

"All. Now. The current will do the rest." *If we get the rest of the gates open.* Again, he wondered how many locks the downstream crew had opened.

The three of them got to it, walked a barrel to the gunnel, blood sloshing over the sides, splashing them, making the deck slippery beneath their feet. Standing on either side, Roger and Patsy tipped it against the gunnel while Dewey squatted and lifted and the three of them heaved it over the side.

They moved on to the next and the next.

The Acton Lock hove into view.

Quincy's heart sank.

Floaters lined the lock, mute sentinels watching their approach with soulless, fish-pale eyes.

Quincy eased off the throttle. The barrels were overboard. The blood would draw the floaters as it flowed downstream . . . eventually. The passage would be much quicker with all the locks open, the water from the Grand Central and the upper reaches of the Regent's flooding into the basin below. The rush of so much water was sure to hasten the delivery of the living dead to the hooligan army waiting at the Regent's Canal Dock. He had no way of knowing if their counterparts working up the canal had opened the lower locks, but one thing was certain—if they failed to open the locks, there would be a bottleneck and no matter what happened in the basin, the canal would remain infested.

Abandoning the mission was not an option. Besides, he thought, looking at the reef of floaters flanking the barge on either side, he had a nasty feeling there would be more of them waiting if they tried for the streets.

Roger and Patsy looked at him for direction. Dewey appeared fascinated by their welcoming committee.

"Get ready, men."

"We're going in?" Patsy's voice was ratcheted up an octave higher than normal. Once it would have tickled his heart to hear fear in the Dove Rower's voice. Instead, it was a reminder to keep his own nerves in check and his voice steady.

"Grab your weapons and hold onto something!"

Quincy increased the throttle. The barge sluggishly picked up speed.

"He's going to ram it!" Dewey shouted. The big man's voice had also risen a notch.

"Roger, pin Newt down so he don't go flying."

The lock with its closed gate and coterie of the waiting dead flew toward them.

Silently, he hoped the lock was full.

***

From the wheelhouse, George Fish watched the struggle taking place on the barge. On the one hand, it was

82

imperative they reach the Regent's Canal Dock by high water. They might never be thanked—the press and politicians certainly would show no gratitude to the flotsam of London society, even if they believed hooligans, costermongers and street urchins were capable of saving the city. Assuming they were successful. Failure was a moot point, as they'd all be dead or on the run.

On the other, as much as he loathed some of the guys on the barge, they, at least, belonged to the same race as he—street rats all, who had learned to survive—even thrive—in the belly of the Beast. It galled him to leave them to such a grisly death . . . only they wouldn't die, would they? And the living would have to kill them all over again when they arrived at the basin.

George strained to see who were among the survivors. Big Dirk Bogart was still standing, bashing away with his deadly shillelagh. Around him were five others. With the dark and the mist and the distance it was hard to tell, but one tall fellow might have been his mate, Roy Munt.

"Heppel!" he barked, turning toward the slope-shouldered tug skipper.

The older man's attention was torn between steering the tug between the boats and barges anchored on either side of the channel and craning his neck to see what was going on in their wake.

"You're thinking of turning back. A rescue mission," the man said reading his mind.

"Can you do it?"

"'Course I can. Thought you were in a hurry to get to Limehouse."

"Any way you can pick up those boys and still get to Limehouse on time?"

"It'll be tight."

"Can you do it?"

"One way to find out."

Expecting Heppel to turn the boat around, George grabbed a handrail, but Heppel eased the throttle instead. Where before the tug was cutting through the water at a good clip, its speed keeping it steady, it now slowed. He felt the roll of the river under him. Any slower and the tug would wallow.

Out the rear window, he saw with alarm the barge was gaining on them.

"Yell down to Humphry to man the winch and take up the slack!"

"The barge is going to ram us!" George yelled back.

"It will if you keep standing there! Relay my order!"

Swallowing the impulse to tell the old man where he could relay his order, George opened the door onto the cold and damp and shouted down to Heppel's deckhand. Skinny Bob Humphry jumped to it and within seconds the slack in the hawser was reeling in.

"Enough!" Heppel yelled. "Leave some slack for maneuvering."

The barge with its beleaguered heroes was closing fast. "It's going to hit us!"

"It won't."

True to his word, Heppel teased the throttle. The barge closed but at a slower rate.

The men on the barge—now there were only four, and it did his heart good to see that one was, indeed, Roy Munt—had seen them. Busy fighting off the creatures grabbing and snapping at them, they snuck desperate glances at the men on the tug's stern.

At the last possible moment, Heppel spun the helm

hard to port and threw the throttle into reverse so the boat churned to a stop then lurched backwards in a great wash of river water. For a terrifying moment, it appeared the craft was in danger of being breached as he exposed the tug's hull to the prow of the barge, but instantly he increased the throttle and hauled hard to port and the tug surged forward just as the barge made contact. The starboard side lifted dangerously, and the tug was pushed sideways taking water over its port gunnel. The men clung to the rail as their feet went out from under them. Heppel held his course and increased throttle for a tick to push back against the barge until the tug righted. The captain held the wheel slightly to starboard to keep the tug snug against the barge.

George grabbed the fire axe from its cradle on the side of the wheelhouse, sprinted across the deck and, leaping from the stern rail, was the first man on the barge.

***

The impact of the canal boat slamming into the wooden gates lifted Quincy in the air and threw him backwards. Only by clinging to the tiller did he keep from being flung over the stern. The tiller wrenched sideways but the prow ground between the gates and squealed to a halt. Quincy revved the throttle and the craft lurched forward and stopped, wedged between the gates.

To his immense relief, the lock was full. The bow rested in water instead of dangling six-feet in the air. But before he could form a plan, they were under attack.

A male floater leapt onto the roof of the engine

house, landed at a crouch, knees bent, arms extended. Despite the bloat and the missing eye and the way its cheeks drooped like melted cheese over its jowls, there was something athletic in its landing, and Quincy wondered if the man in the ruined blue shirt had been a sportsman. Did these things retain some memory of their former existence?

The creature rose, its fogged eye glowed in the dim light as it bared its lips in a silent snarl and started toward him. Then it sank to its knees, a hatchet buried in its head. Roger rammed his foot in the now lifeless cadaver's back and wrenched his weapon free.

"Help Patsy open the lower gate," Quincy shouted. "Then head for the Old Ford Lock. Stay off the towpath, take the streets."

Roger didn't hesitate, but turned and, leaping from the engine house, brought his hatchet down on the neck of a floater coming over the gunnel, spun and took out another's knee. Dewey, with his staff held horizontally before him, rushed two more floaters to the bow and drove them into the water. With the windlass shoved through his wide belt and his crooked teeth bared in a grimace, Patsy swung his staff taking out the feet of a floater on the dock, then, using the gunnel as a springboard, leapt onto the platform and sprinted toward the lock mechanism. A born footballer, Patsy sidestepped and ducked his shoulders, eluding grabbing hands. Roger was right behind him, chopping arms and faces.

Rog knew what he was about. He would open as many locks as he could for as long as he could.

Jumping down from the engine house, Quincy scooped up the cooper's hammer Roger earlier used to open barrels. He knelt beside Newt . The boy didn't look so well. His teeth were clenched in a rictus of pain. Bloodshot eyes glowed like red moons in a grey face. Quincy recognized imminent death: he could smell it on him, as he'd smelled it on back-alley gin rats and, once, on a deep-cut kid bleeding out on the sidewalk.

"Take this," he said, shoving the hammer into his hand. He didn't know if Newt heard, the lad stared right through him . . . as if seeing whatever the dying saw before the reaper took them. "I'm gonna be busy."

It felt like desertion leaving the wounded boy to fend for himself, even if he was a member of a rival gang. But true to his word, he was instantly engaged in combat.

Shirtless, with arms like tree trunks, a chest that—even though flayed raw by the canal bottom—still rippled with muscle, the floater reaching for him had the physique of a prizefighter. Quincy rolled, came up in a fighting stance and drove a left into the creature's jaw. Teeth flew but its head hardly moved. Was the fucking thing grinning at him?

He whipped out his chopper, an eight-inch Afrikaner Bowie his uncle brought back from the Boer War, and drove it into the thing's temple. Or tried to. True to his prediction, the creature blocked the knife-wielding arm with its left forearm, stepped inside his guard and delivered a teeth-rattling uppercut that lifted Quincy off his feet.

Quincy scuttled back, shook his head to clear it and crouched with the knife before him. He had a loose tooth of his own. He spat it out. Guard up, the floater came at him. They did remember something of their past existence! This one was advancing with its fists up and its head down as if it were in the square ring battling for prize money.

He didn't have time for this! Other floaters were boarding!

Keeping his head low and his elbows close together, he dove inside his opponent's guard, shoved both hands up and out to drive the creature's arms wide and delivered a head-butt that was rewarded with a satisfying *crack* as his hairline rammed under the thing's chin, snapping its head back and toppling it.

He leapt over his rival, swept the chopper nearly beheading a second attacker. Dewey was on the lock slashing and shoving his way through the crowd with his two-handed staff. Quincy sheathed his knife, grabbed Newt's staff and followed, thrusting and kicking, covering the big man's back as they progressed.

Out of the corner of his eye, Quincy saw Newt pass. The boy was walking, head thrust forward, eyes straight ahead, as if intent on helping Roger and Patsy open the gates. He gripped the cooper's hammer. Quincy started to call out, but the boy was gone, lost in the press.

10

THE TUG WAS APPROACHING, lights ablaze, barge in tow. Habitually straight-faced, Will couldn't help cracking a grin. He exchanged glances with Foley, Drummond, and Budge. Their smiles matched his own.

The tide was at its peak. Both the lower and upper gates to the barge lock were open. The water had risen nearly a foot in the basin as the river flowed in. The river was dark, the fog building, but as the tug drew closer, Will saw through the spyglass the floaters in the water. A chill ran through him. The water around the tug and barge swarmed with the living dead. Though he saw no sign of stroking arms, of kicking feet, they kept pace, surrounding the vessels like a flotilla of monstrous fish.

So many!

He turned the glass to the tug. The bow was lined with London's youth. Among them, big Dirk Bogart stood out. He'd lost his bowler and his unruly mane corkscrewed in all directions, reminding Will of that Greek monster woman, Medusa, with snakes for hair. A couple lads were waving, as if hoping they'd been spotted and the lock was open. Skimming the glass along the gunnel, he saw no sign of floaters. He turned his attention to the barge and the hairs on his head bristled with a thrill of supernatural horror. The deck was crowded with the animated dead, gazing blindly forward as if alerted by some silent communication they'd reached their destination and dinner was about to be served. Cadavers lay scattered about the deck, proof the barge had been the scene of an epic struggle.

Will passed the glass to Foley. To Drummond and Budge, he said, "Let's go." He continued as they descended the stair, "Soon as they're in, close the gates. And start the pumps. It'll take time to fill the basin."

And in that time, he thought, it would be hell keeping the floaters in the water.

So many!

***

George Fish stared out the wheelhouse window as Captain Heppel steered the tug into the arc-lighted glare of the Regent's Canal Dock. Rows of great square-riggers lay anchored in the middle of the basin. Steam colliers lined the jetties where cranes towered over the coal bunkers. It was good to see armed chaps lining the quays and jetties. They would have their work cut out for them and no mistake.

"We made it!" he said, releasing a sigh he hadn't realized he'd been holding in. His arms ached from carving his way through the floaters aboard the barge. To Heppel's credit, the tug captain had kept the boat hard against the barge while they fought so when the path was clear, the survivors could climb over the gunnel to safety. They'd lost not a single man. Dirk Bogart, his own Roy Munt, and two Wandsworth Scuttlers, Small Tom and Eustace Pye, had made it back to the tug along with the lads who had jumped to their assistance.

"Of course we made it!" Heppel said contemptuously without looking at his passenger. "Ya think I was taking you for a joy ride? I earn my pay and don't you forget it, you dundering milksop!"

Fish was in too good a mood to take offense. "I won't forget and you'll get your pay, assuming anybody's alive after tonight."

Heppel snorted. "Since when did you become the philosopher? Gor, what a waste of good mutton!" he added as the tug plowed through sheep carcasses." The old man shook his head, but he was grinning. "Is that the plan? Feed the bogles till they get so fat they explode. Looks like you're not the only nincompoop out tonight!"

For the most part, the plan was working. Sure enough, the "bogles" were battening on the carcasses, tearing into the bloody meat and shaking their heads like terriers in a rat pit. Not all were so easily satisfied. Even as Fish watched, others, perhaps drawn to warm blood by some sixth sense, were swarming out of the water onto the docks where lads were busy shoving them back or laying iron to skulls.

"You say the plan is to flood the basin with oil and set the bogles afire?" Heppel said, cutting the engine.

"That's the plan."

"Well, I volunteered to deliver you to Limehouse, not stay and watch my livelihood burn! Tell Humphry to release the barge."

"Aye, Captain!" Fish gave a mock salute and headed out of the wheelhouse, fire axe in hand. The broad blade dripped liquid corruption. His outfit was drenched with brains and splattered entrails and he couldn't wait to get back to his digs and into fresh togs.

When he reached the deck, he saw the deckhand had anticipated Heppel's order. The power winch whirred as it hauled in the slack on the tow line. Suddenly the winch jammed. Humphry tried to crank it manually, but it was stuck. Ned Meadows lent a hand and Small Tom and Eustace Pye grabbed the hawser and started pulling.

The slack was below the water. Fish could figure what was weighing it.

"Move aside," he said and raised his axe.

***

Patsy nearly had the paddles open. Though Roger stood behind him laying about with his hatchet, providing a measure of protection as he cranked the windlass, his skin crawled. He was exposed and expected at any moment to feel cold hands grip his shoulders, icy teeth sink into his flesh.

He sensed a hush in the shuffling of feet on the flagstones but was intent on completing his task and didn't look up till he heard Roger speak.

"Newt!"

He glanced up eager to see that Newt had not succumbed to his wound but had come to help them. Instead, he turned just in time to see Newt swing the cooper's hammer.

The steel struck Roger square in the forehead, cracking his skull. The City Roader spasmed as he dropped to his knees then collapsed on his face.

Newt stepped over his fallen comrade. A wild light played in his bloodshot eyes. His lips stretched in a feral snarl. There was no sign of recognition in his eyes, no mercy as he raised the hammer and Patsy flung up his arm.

The blow never landed. Newt was shoved out of the way as Dewey Haines appeared, driving the dead before him. Quincy, likewise armed with a quarterstaff, was right behind him.

"Open the gate!" Quincy roared as he smashed skulls.

Patsy shoved the key lock through his belt and, ducking through the crowd, threw his weight against the balance beam that opened the lower gates. The paddles weren't completely open, however, and the resistance of the water made the beam difficult to move. Then Dewey was beside him, backing into the beam as he fought off floaters, adding his considerable strength. The gates moved, then they swept open and the lock water spilled into the canal below.

***

The dock was chaos. Everywhere scenes of horror and bravery played out under the harsh lights. Frank Peck, as if every floater that climbed onto the quay was personally responsible for killing his brother, cleaved a path before him with his iron wrecking bar. On either side of the big guy, Ralph Bailey and Harry Hodd did killing work. Behind them, Will and Foley and Alby Budge's weapons rose and fell. But for every floater downed two more took its place. The scene reminded Will of the Battle of Rorke's Drift from the Zulu wars, a story every man, woman and child in England knew. A hundred and fifty British troops, outnumbered forty to one, resisted between 3,000 and 4,000 Zulu warriors who attacked the former trading post in wave after wave for twelve hours.

The water churned with sheep carcasses and floaters, but more and more, as the oil spread its greasy sheen over the basin, the undead swarmed onto the quays and jetties attacking defenders. Will felt for the flare gun thrust through his belt. For the plan to work, the water in the basin had to be covered in fuel oil. Bill Drummond, Alvin Pott and Nate Dunham were doing all they could at the pumping station; but there were over five acres of water and the pumps could empty the tanks only so fast.

The crane operators were swinging the coal grab-buckets attached to the ends of the boom cables to sweep floaters back into the water. Closed, the huge iron jaws did double duty as battering rams. From the wild grins on their faces, the stevedores looked to be having a jolly time.

The tug had dropped the survivors off on the steam quay by Horseferry Road. Two of his Lads, Jake Longhill and Rob Younger, hadn't made it. The news hit hard. He'd known them all his life. Now they were gone. Like Tim Peck.

Maybe not gone.

For a flash, he saw them shambling, their waistcoats and trousers streaming water, their faces pale and pocked, their fingers grasping.

Scratch that. With Bogart and his shillelagh on board, it wasn't likely they'd be returning. He supposed he should be grateful to the New Cut chief for that at least. Anger clenched his jaw at the thought. "We'll mourn them later," he muttered under his breath.

"What's that?" Foley asked beside him. The policeman had emptied his Webley and was using a spike maul he'd taken from a fallen warrior. A glistening ichor dripped from the elongated double head.

"Said we'll mourn our dead tomorrow," he repeated, raising his voice as he dispatched a noseless ghoul. "If we live the night."

"Speak for yourself," the constable said and caved in a floater's skull before continuing. "I don't plan on dying just yet."

****

After dropping his passengers off, Captain Heppel and his deckhand Bob Humphry made straight for the barge lock but found the gate closed.

"Son of a bitch!" Heppel growled through his beard. The lock swarmed with bogles. They milled about looking as vagrant and disreputable as a gang of Calcutta beggars.

He steered the helm hard astarboard to avoid ramming the gate. Immediately a loud *clunk-clunk-clunk* rose from below. The tug slowed. He tried increasing the throttle. Gears ground, stopped.

Jammed! Something—sheep's carcass, bogle—had fouled the propeller. The *Mary Belle* was adrift.

As the tug slid past the lock, close enough to look into the dead eyes of the bogles, two of the creatures turned and walked straight for the boat, dropping off the platform and splashing into the water as if expecting to walk onto the tug.

Heppel had been in tight places. Smuggling liquor from Holland in his youth, knowing the Queen's excise men would have you thrown in jail or sent to Australia if you got caught. A stint on a blockade runner delivering supplies, mail and ordinance to the

Confederacy during the hostilities. There were times when the hairs on his neck tingled with the thought of the hangman's noose lowering over his head. But never had his skin crawled with such pure bug crazy horror than at the sight of those bogles turning their dead eyes on him.

He was adrift in a sea of hungry dead. And the oil was spreading around the *Mary Belle*'s hull. How long till the lads fired the basin? He rubbed a sweaty hand over the back of his neck as the realization sank in that he was going to have to put in somewhere and take his chances on shore and his boat—his livelihood—was going to go up in flames.

Bob Humphry's scream shattered his thoughts.

He froze, and for a moment heard nothing but the pounding of his rebellious heart. Then he remembered Bob Humphry was his responsibility and started toward the wheelhouse door.

The door rattled.

He stopped.

"Bob?"

For answer, the door rattled harder. Then a sound like nails scraping down the metal put his teeth on edge. He backed away as a one-eyed horror stared through the window.

Pain slammed up his left arm. Clutching his chest with his right hand, he backed into a corner until he felt the steel wall behind him. He slid down its surface until he was sitting.

His last thought before the pain, transcending the bounds of the wheelhouse, encompassed London, Europe, the world, the stars, and then, as if in an instant, like the snuffing of a candle, became a speck of calm, was if he remained silent and made himself as small as possible, perhaps the bogles would not find him.

***

Quincy's staff was a blur of strikes and thrusts as he kept the floaters at bay. His blood was up, his senses keen. He breathed through clenched teeth as he leaned into his blows. He felt tireless, exhilarated, a machine that has run for hours and can run for hours still. He heard the roar of falling water as the lock spilled into the canal below. He didn't look but felt a stab of pride. They'd done it! The lock was open! Whether they'd make it to the next lock was uncertain, but this one was open, blood and floaters carried downstream by the surge!

A moan, as if from some great gored beast, rose above the roar of cascading water. The pressing dead paused and turned their heads. The canal boat, wedged midship between the gates, was tilting, the bow dropping with the falling water. The stern lifted high into the air, a tilted column silhouetted against the sky, then the surge caught it under the bow and the whole thing shot out of the lock and raced down the canal, taking a stream of floaters with it.

Quincy glanced back to see how Dewey and Patsy were faring but saw no sign of them. Whether they'd made it off the lock or lay murdered behind the floaters that blocked his view, he had no way of knowing.

He was surrounded now. Alone. He crushed the skull of the nearest creature, jabbed another in the throat, gripped the staff in both hands and tried to plow his way to the street. But they were too many.

Hands ripped the staff from his grasp. Others

seized his arms. Rage vied with terror as he struggled in their cold embrace. One dug its nails into his cheek and throat and drew his face closer to its own, its dead breath mingling with his. Maws battened onto his throat, his face, his wrists.

The kiss of their teeth was ice.

11

T WAS AMAZING JUST how much energy fear could give you. It could shut you down so you gave up and curled up in a ball and let the terror take you. Or you could seize it, slap reins on it and ride it into the maelstrom. Kate's skin tingled as if her nerves had risen to the surface and her senses were hyperacute. Objects—fence-boards, roofs, chimneys etched against the sky, the ripple of reflected light upon dark water— all seemed sharply defined as if outlined by a pale yet luminous light. She was near jogging, but nowhere near tired.

They had lost one in the fray. Bev Bennet, of Queen Jane's brood. And Nell Quigley had succumbed. They'd left her in a warehouse doorway, telling Annie Dawes, her Dove Row mate, they'd be back for her, though Kate had a creeping suspicion she wouldn't be there when they returned.

She heard the flood before she saw it. A tumultuous rumble like logs rolling down a flight of stairs or a lashing wind driving torrential rain. Her gaze swept up the canal. In the distance, the Great Eastern Railway trestle carved a black arch over the water. At first, she thought the trestle was falling, granite blocks and steel rails plunging into the channel; then she saw the wave of rolling foam squeeze between the abutments cresting several feet above the canal's normal height.

Then the water was roaring by, the surge splashing over the path. They scurried back. Water washed over their feet. In the current were figures, some flailing as if trying to swim against the hurtling tide, others splayed like starfish upon the foam pinwheeling downstream.

Kate's heart leapt. Several girls cried out, their joy palpable in the smoke-tainted air. The men who'd gone upstream had succeeded! The upper locks were open, the unfettered waters sweeping down to the basin! The canal's cargo of floaters hurled downstream upon the flood!

As they paused to watch the shoals of living dead sweep past, several eyes stared upstream—Winnie Tuttle, Mary Haines and Annie Dawes among them. Kate knew what was utmost in their thoughts. These girls had skin in the game. Though no Lambeth Lad accompanied the heroes that had gone ahead to open the locks—the Lads were at the basin helping Will— these had friends and kin on the barge. Though there was bad blood between the gangs, Kate hoped they were all right.

"Look!" Mary Haines cried out.

A narrowboat shot out of the dark beneath the trestle and in a moment was sweeping by. The boat was crewless, its deck abandoned. Annie's cry was audible over the watery rush.

"Oh, God, no!" Winnie shook her head as she watched the barge vanish downstream.

Kate's heart sank. She shared their anxiety, knew how she would feel if Will had been on that barge and she was watching it hurtle crewless downstream. Her thoughts turned to the basin. The canal was carrying the floaters straight to Will. More would be coming in from the river. She could only hope he would survive, that she would see him again, alive after tonight, as she watched the boat disappear into the distance.

***

George Fish, Ned Meadows and Roy Munt observed an uneasy truce with Dirk Bogart, Jeb Wilkes and Wandsworth Scuttlers, Small Tom and Eustace Pye, as they took a stand to battle an endless stream of living dead.

Pye had fallen, but Small Tom, his Wandsworth mate, fought on. Using brass knuckles no less. George, whose axe rose and fell spraying brains and severing limbs with every stroke, knew the little fucker was a scrapper who liked close combat, but that was for money, pride or revenge. This was something else. The lad was thoroughly enjoying himself. The crazed smile on his face, his knuckles dripping gore, was guaranteed to terrify even the most hardened Londoner.

And people think I'm crazy! George thought, admiring the little warrior.

The dead possessed some glimmer of consciousness, for, once the boys learned the hard way the undead couldn't be stopped by gutting them or ramming a pry rod through their chest and only crushing the skull or driving a rod into their brain stopped them, some of the undead had resorted to dropping low and going for the takedown like wrestlers.

As one did now.

A big brute, the creature still had its nose and two

eyes and moved more agilely than the bloated sausages that had spent more time in the water. George, no mean wrestler himself—though he preferred belt and knife and detested rolling in the dust like a common urchin—leapt back so the grasping paws missed his knees and brought the axe down severing the creature's spine. But the quay was slimed with blood and spilled organs and his feet slipped out from under him. He landed on top of his opponent.

As George tried to shove himself to his feet, knowing full well the creature, even with half its body disabled, was dangerous, a shadow fell over him. Squinting against the glare of arc light, he saw Dirk Bogart raise his shillelagh. George lifted a hand defensively. Son of a bitch if the bastard wasn't using the occasion to settle old debts!

***

The quay was more crowded than Lambeth Walk on a Saturday night and more boisterous. But not with pedestrians. No leather-lunged proprietor shouting "Bravo!" when a crack shot rings the bell and bears off a coconut. No hand cart pushers hawking eel pies or books or sheet music or toffee, butchers' meat, shoes, coats, buttons, or cure for the toothache. No good-humored, pleased-with-himself drunk out for a stroll and on the lookout for anything not nailed down. No mothers pushing strollers or corner organ grinder with his coterie of dancing children. No cocky young men with their bowlers aslant giving the girls a wink. No shouts of "Hot eels! Nice hot eels!" No welcome cry from the pea soup seller of "Warm your hands and fill your bellies for a halfpenny." No smells of fried fish or roasted chestnuts.

No, all was lurching, clutching horror. All rising and falling weapons and fountaining corruption. Infernal visions that reeked of the ignoble and ignominious terminus of life.

Will moved through a dreamlike reality that defied any notion of sanity, a waking nightmare in which creatures from the darkest imagination stretched taloned hands and tore life from the living.

Glancing up in a moment's reprieve, Will saw the octagonal accumulator tower rearing above the heads of the teeming combatants and knew the oil tanks were close. The wind was rising, bringing with it the smell of London burning. Glowering clouds mounted in the west, their underbellies glowing dark red from reflected firelight. The city stood as much in danger of ravaging by fire as by the plague of the undead. Would the flames consume the city as they had in the Great Fire over two-hundred years ago when a gale-force wind carried sparks and burning embers block to block, neighborhood to neighborhood, so by the time the wind died and the fire exhausted itself, half the city was cinders?

Ahead of him, Frank Peck, covered in gore, cut a path through the dead clambering out of the blood-and-oil-fouled water. Did the big guy ever tire? Will no longer felt his arms and breathing had become a labored in-out through clenched teeth and every step a hard-won victory. He envied his friend's anger. He'd never managed to stay mad at anyone for long. Get even, move on. Watch your back but otherwise forget about it. Life was too short and dwelling on yesterday's injustices spoiled today's opportunities.

He heard a cry—one among many. It took him a

moment to realize Alby Budge was missing. He looked back and saw the Bow Commoner thrashing on the quay under the weight of three floaters. He tried to reach him, but the thrashing stopped and the press of combatants bore him along.

***

They were coming up on the Twig Folly Bridge when Razor Lil stopped and pointed into the darkness. "Someone's coming."

Sure enough, two wet and bedraggled shapes emerged onto the towpath.

Only two to kill, Kate thought, tightening her grip on her pry bar. Though kill didn't really apply to the already dead. Destroy then.

Other girls raised their weapons.

"Wait!" Mary Haines yelled. "Dewey?"

"Hello, Mar!" the taller of the approaching figures called as nonchalantly as if they were met in the park on a summer's day.

Kate saw the resemblance as the boy came closer. He and Mary were both blue-eyed and blond. Dewey had Mary's broad shoulders, broader. His big hands looked as if they could bend pry bars. Her brother and make no mistake. And the other?

Annie Dawes supplied the answer. She looked at the swarthy, surly-looking youth, then past him at the trestle entrance, as if expecting more company.

"Patsy . . . where's Jimmy?" she said, her voice faltering, as if she already knew the answer.

Kate recalled the girl had a brother.

Winnie Tuttle stepped forward. "And Quincy and Roger?"

The young men exchanged a glance. Dewey stared

stoically; his expression conveyed the bad news. Their clothing still clung to them but wasn't dripping. They'd been in the water then, but out of it for a bit.

Sorrow and anger vied for dominance of Patsy's expression as he delivered the news. "He didn't make it, Annie."

"And Newt?"

Patsy shook his head. His grimace, along with the crewless narrow boat, told Kate how their night had gone. He turned to Winnie. "Roger's gone. That's certain. And last we saw, Quincey was surrounded."

Winnie Tuttle's forehead turned thunderous. "You deserted him?"

Dewey broke in. "We had no choice. We couldn't help and we still had to open the Ford Road Lock—which we did!"

Instead of crying for her lost brother, Annie Dawes put on a fierce face and gripped her blade. "Kill them all!" she snarled. "Doesn't matter they're already dead!"

"Looks like we'll get the chance," Ruby Morton said.

Kate followed her gaze. A posse of floaters were coming up the path. Seeing the girls, they quickened their pace.

"Come on," Patsy Kennedy said. "I've got an idea."

***

The knobbed end of the blackthorn club missed George Fish's head by inches and stove in the floater's skull. The creature spasmed, then lay still.

Grinning savagely, gold tooth twinkling under the arc light, Bogart extended a hand. George took it and Bogart heaved him to his feet.

"You owe me," Bogart said. His tone was good-humored as if he'd stood the Elephant and Castle chief a beer at McNally's, but the glint in his eye was vicious.

Before George could decide whether to thank the New Cut captain or tell him he owed him a kick in the arse, a great roar like the rumble of an approaching train rose from the direction of the Regent's Canal. The concrete trembled beneath their feet. As their gaze sought the source, a wave surged over the Commercial Street Lock and rolled across the basin. The big ships rose and dropped, wallowing as the wave passed beneath their great hulls, their masts leaning dangerously before righting. Then the wave dashed over them and human and floater alike were swept into the water.

***

Floaters tumbled on the face of the wave as it surged across the basin. Will had a moment to think, *They did it!* Quincy Bird's crew . . . Kate and her band of Amazons . . . had succeeded in opening the locks and the canal was flushing the floaters into the basin!

Then the wave was across the basin, crashing into the sea wall and returning. Will pivoted to duck behind a shed but the wave washed over him, knocked him off his feet. When it fell back into the basin, it dragged him in.

He sank, tumbled heels over head as he was borne under. All was roaring darkness, confusion and terror. He surfaced, gasping and sputtering, the taste of oil and fouler stuff thick in his throat. He was in the water! He'd lost his weapon and he was in the water!

With *them!*

Something bumped him and panic surged as he

thought a floater was about to seize him. But it was a sheep's carcass, the meat cold and slimy under his hand. He shoved it away.

He wasn't the greatest swimmer and he trashed about as he searched for the dock. Then he saw their faces, their eyes just above the water. Those that had eyes. They had no trouble swimming but glided toward him as if they were as immaterial as ghosts or wisps of fog.

A hand grabbed his ankle, yanked him under. Startled, he gulped air before the water closed over his head. Terror seized his heart as light receded and darkness grew. He kicked with his free leg. His heel struck something solid—again, and again—as bubbles escaped his nose and his lungs burned. The hand released him. He kicked for the surface, but a hand seized his other ankle, pulled him back. Motes of white light swam in his vision.

He looked down. Below and all around him, the fish-pale faces emerged from the dark, their rictus snarls showing teeth unnaturally long. Clawed hands stretched toward him.

Beside him, something plunged into the water. A hand grabbed his arm.

***

Dirk Bogart spat greasy water when George Fish pulled him onto the dock. George had lost his maul. He was amazed the New Cut boss still clutched his shillelagh. Did the man sleep with the bloody thing?

With his wild blood-lusting eyes and savage snarl, his wet hair plastered over his forehead, the man could have been mistaken for one of their attackers.

"Guess we're even," George said in a pleasant voice

he might have used had they played a game of chess to a draw. A voice guaranteed to rile the New Cut ruffian.

Bogart moved so fast George barely had time to react. The shillelagh came whistling toward his face. He ducked and it passed over his shoulder.

Burying its knobbed end in a floater's forehead.

Bogart's gold tooth winked. "Not by a long shot!"

***

Will broke the surface, gasping and sputtering. He struggled to free himself, but the arm clasped across his chest was strong.

"Be still. I've got you," a voice he recognized as Foley's commanded.

The police constable was pulling him toward the quay. He struggled with the humiliation of being saved by a policeman. He hoped no one saw. He'd be the butt of a thousand jokes from Wandsworth to Limehouse if they did. Of course, he'd be dead or worse had the constable not come after him.

Remembering the pocked faces drifting toward him out of the inky depths, he thrashed about looking for attackers.

"Be still!"

Immediately he saw one, its matted forelocks plastered over eyes like fogged mirrors. A pale hand reached for him. He kicked it in the face. Still it came on. He kicked it again.

Then Foley was shoving him onto the quay.

"Go!" Foley barked.

Will hauled himself out. No easy going—fouled with oil, the concrete was slippery as an eel.

Foley was in trouble. Holding the monster at bay with one hand while paddling with the other to keep his head above water wasn't working. As if the thing knew it had the advantage, it pulled him under.

Will dug a hobnailed boot into a joint in the concrete, reached down, grabbed the creature's arm and pulled. It snapped at his hand. He released it, grabbed it by the back of its shirt collar. Foley broke loose, hauled himself onto the dock and seized its other arm. Together they dragged it from the water and while Will pinned it chest down to the quay with his knee, Foley lifted his boot and smashed his heel into its skull. For a moment they stood over the ruined remains, panting as they took stock of the damage.

"You bit?" Foley asked.

The question surprised Will. He hadn't thought about it. He gave himself a quick once over, patting arms and face.

"No. You?"

"I'm good. Look!" Foley gestured toward the jury-rigged system of oil pipes Drummond and his boys had rigged. The flood had knocked the pipes askew, rupturing the hastily sealed joints, and fuel was spewing over the quay, washing around their boots.

Will reached for the flare gun, fearing he'd lost it. He hadn't. He pulled it from his belt. Water streamed from the wide barrel. Would it work?

12

THE DESTRUCTOR LAY BETWEEN a chemical plant and a barge works. The cluster of ornate brick buildings, stabling, and cart yard covered an acre. A one-hundred-eighty-foot chimney towered over the complex. Like the sawmill, the destructor was silent tonight, its furnaces cold, the great crushing cylinders that pulverized the parish waste before incinerating it over the flames still.

Patsy led them up an inclined roadway to the tipping platform in the main building's second floor where, during normal operation, cart after cart of house, trade, and street refuse is tipped into the feeders. In the crusher, refuse is ground between massive rotating cylinders until it is of a uniform consistency, after which it is burned over a 2,000-degree fire. Nothing goes to waste. The clinkers are crushed to suitable size for roadway and footpath foundation or ground even finer in the mortar mill for mortar and cement. The burning process produces steam which, in turn, powers generators to supply the works with electricity for light and for the operation of the pulverizers and mills.

The floaters—over two dozen of them: they'd picked up more on the run—were at the bottom of the roadway by the time they got to the top.

"Here," Patsy said, pulling a lever that raised a steel door set into the floor of the platform.

Kate looked into the feed hole, but it was dark down there and she could make out nothing of the destructor's workings. She got it that Patsy wanted to lure the floaters into the hole, but how? She glanced back. The creatures were already coming up. And quickly.

"How do we get them to jump into this hole?" Queen Jane asked. The Forty Elephants sovereign's look of incredulity matched Kate's.

For answer, Patsy slammed his fist against a green button mounted on the wall beside the feeder hole. The other was red. Immediately a rumbling welled up through the concrete floor. Kate felt the vibrations through the soles of her boots as massive machinery started up below.

"No time to fire the furnace," Patsy explained, his sour mug frowning at the mob halfway up the ramp. "The crushers ought to do the job." He turned to the girls, addressed them collectively. "Stay here, on this side of the feeder. Any come around the sides," he indicated the narrow passage to either side of the feeder hole, "shove them in. I'll try to get them to come straight on."

"How're you—?"

But he was gone, running down the incline toward the living dead.

"He's crazy!" the Bow Commoner twins, Fanny and Alice Dupree, said in unison.

"Yeah, but he's quick," said Patsy's gang mate Annie Dawes.

Sure enough, the wiry Dove Rower sprinted to the

lead floater and kicked him in the chest, so he went down and two following on his heels spilled over him. Heading back up the ramp, Patsy moved more slowly, letting them keep close on his heels till he was near the open feed door. At the last instant, he broke into a sprint and leapt across the chasm.

In close pursuit, the floaters at the head of the mob tumbled into the hole. The sound coming up through the trap door changed. To the deafening roar of steel on steel was added the noise of crunching bone and bursting flesh. The pressure from those behind drove those ahead into the pit. The creatures went silently to their second deaths. No sign of startlement showed in their eyes as they dropped into the chasm. They made no outcry. Only the incessant roar of the pulverizing cylinders and the gruesome crunching and splattering of mangled bodies assaulted the ears of the living.

There was a moment when the noise faltered, as the cylinders, glutted with a surfeit of corpses, caught and strained, but only a moment; then, with a great lurch and crunch and a geyser of meat and reeking putrescence that shot up above the feed hole and fell back into the chasm with a nauseous *splash*, the rollers freed themselves and the roaring continued.

***

Would it work? The flare gun was soaked! The cartridge wet!

The gusting wind plastered Will's soaked shirt to his body. Thunder rumbled in the distance. Again, he thought of the wind fanning the city's flames, the fire consuming block after block, devouring rich and poor neighborhoods alike. But London would fend for itself.

It had risen from the ashes before. Besides, he had his hands full at the moment.

Floaters clambered onto the quay. Others, already on the dock, were coming for them.

Will's finger curled around the trigger. It occurred to him that, with Foley and himself covered in oil and fuel flowing around their boots, he might not be in the best position to light up the basin. He backed away from the water's edge searching for dry ground. The nearby sheds wouldn't do—they housed the oil tanks.

Foley dodged a floater, slipped and went down hard. The floater fell on him. The constable had his hands full keeping the beast from sinking its snapping teeth into his face. Will aimed the pistol at the floater, but Foley and his attacker were both covered in oil. He risked setting the policeman ablaze if he fired.

In that moment of hesitation, a floater seized him by the shoulder, spun him around. He stared into its murderous gaze as they tumbled to the quay. His back slammed into the concrete and the gun went off.

Will's heart sank as he watched the white trail stream into the sky. He'd wasted their only chance to set the basin ablaze. But he was too busy to bemoan his failure. Discarding the gun, he used both hands to fend off the creature struggling to savage his throat. His attacker was female. Despite the decay, she looked no more than a teen, and a slight one at that. Still, the creature fought with the ferocity of a ravenous beast. For a moment, as her long wet hair draped his face, they stared eye to eye, grimace to grimace, and Will had the horrible impression she was going to kiss him. He shoved her off and had one knee under him when he saw a brilliant white light streaming down.

Wild joy surged through him. He'd shot the flare straight up! It was coming down on the basin! He hadn't wasted it after all!

He gave his attacker a final push and dove for cover.

Whoosh!

Fire raced across the oil-soaked basin setting carcasses—human, floaters, sheep—ablaze, sped over the quay and shot up the ruptured pipes. The oil tanks exploded.

Whump!

The blast caught Will in mid-leap, hurled him through the air into a corrugated iron shed.

Darkness took him.

***

Exhausted, Kate sank to her knees before the piled dead, closed her eyes and rested her forehead against the iron pry bar she used to support herself. She felt nothing, not elation of having destroyed their attackers, not the heady rush fear lent in time of danger, not even gratitude for having survived. Just bone-weary, mind-numbing, soul-draining exhaustion.

The battle was over. The dead lay piled on either side of the pit where the revenants had tried to breach the ranks of the living. The first wave of floaters had gone into the feeder, but soon those behind, as if realizing they were shoving those before them to their destruction, broke ranks and forced their way around the sides of the pit where Kate and the girls met them in a final stand.

Some had broken through. These too lay sprawled on the defenders' side of the feeder with staved faces, bashed skulls. Among the felled floaters lay four of her company. She thought of them as hers now. Despite their history of division and the animosities between the rival gangs—animosities that had existed in her parents and grandparents' day—she had fought with these girls, side by side against a relentless and unimaginable foe.

The pulverizer's roar ceased as Patsy punched the red off button and the great crushing cylinders ground to a halt.

No one spoke. No one had breath to spare and what was there to say anyway? They'd done their job. The locks from St. Pancras to Commercial Road were open. Hopefully, most of the Regent's Canal floaters had washed down to the Limehouse Basin. But at what a cost! London burned. But that was remote . . . other people's tragedy that would be felt only when, in days to come, the living walked among the ashes. Here the tragedy was immediate.

Death had visited the Bow Commoner twins. Without knowing them personally Kate didn't know which survived, but one gore-splattered sister knelt on the ground cradling her dead sibling, cooing to her as if she were only ill and would soon revive as tears streamed from her eyes. One of Beth's girls, Samantha "Sam" Crowden, lay nearby, her throat an open wound, the blood wreathing her head running into the feeder. Midge Tibbets had actually gone into the pit, struggling with a floater who had taken the Reaper with it. The indiscriminate pulverizing cylinders had ground her flesh and bone along with that of the undead. Queen Jane's Hatty . . . Razor Lil's Prudence . . .

"Kate." Ruby Morton, her Lambeth mate, laid a trembling hand on her shoulder. Ruby, who cropped her hair short as a boy's as a fighting aid, looked as soul weary as Kate felt.

Kate rose, nodded she was all right. Her arm ached. She couldn't feel the iron bar. She gripped it in both hands as if she might need to swing it again. But when she looked down the ramp, she saw no more of the enemy advancing.

Around her, survivors stood or knelt catching their breath. Mary and Dewey Haines stood like solemn warriors, weapons in hand, surveying the aftermath of battle. New Cut Beth bled from a gash in her forehead. Even Deidre and Mags Goody, for all their brute vitality, looked ready to crumple.

What was left but to take to the streets and head back to the basin where, she prayed, their male counterparts fared better than they.

Patsy Kennedy cleared his throat. With his angry eyes and teeth white against his corpse-stained scowl, he alone of the diminished throng looked as if he still had fight in him. "We'd best get moving," he said to no one in particular.

Queen Jane, used to giving orders, merely nodded.

The assembly jumped when thunder cracked directly overhead. Kate looked up. Immediately a hard rain descended on the corrugated metal roof, the drumming so loud and so sudden she was reminded of the flood that had roared through the Great Eastern Railway trestle and for the second time that night imagined they would be swept away.

***

Will woke in a spasm of coughing, lungs on fire, red light flickering around him. He lay on his back gazing up through reefs of black smoke. The arc lights were out, and though he no longer heard the relentless pounding of the great piston that ran the dock's hydraulic equipment, the basin was by no means silent. Men were yelling, but rather than cries of agony and dismay his ears rang with shouts of triumph.

He tried to stand. The world swayed and he sat down hard. He was on the swing bridge over Narrow Street looking down into the basin. The tall ships were burning. Flames consumed the decks, leapt from the masts. He hoped the sailors had made it ashore. Smoking, twisted metal was all that remained of the oil sheds. Warehouses blazed and, as he watched, the fire reached the timber yards at the north end of the basin, igniting the vast stores of lumber. The coal bins had caught. They would be a long time burning, and with the city ablaze there would be no one to extinguish the fires.

As if reading his thought, Foley said, "On the bright side, the police won't be arresting anyone for arson any time soon."

Preoccupied with his surroundings, Will hadn't noticed his companions. Foley stood beside him along with Frank Peck. Both were liberally splashed with black and red like characters straight out of a painting of hell. He presumed they'd dragged him to safety. He started to work up the spit to thank them but noticed Frank's shirt was torn and a ragged strip of flesh hung from his arm. Will recalled the similar flap of flesh the floater had ripped from Tim Peck's face. His heart sank with the realization Frank would be joining his brother. Remembering the times they'd joked about their wounds returning to the Walk after a clash with a rival gang, he searched for a boisterous quip, but his heart wasn't in it.

"We did it!" Frank said helping Will to his feet. Either Frank didn't understand the transformation he was about to undergo, or he was being stoic—a big grin split his grimed face.

Holding on to the rail, Will watched as here and there across the wide basin man and monster fought. The numbers were greatly reduced—on both sides. So many dead! Come morning there would be grieving aplenty. Still, the triumphant cheers that went up as London's heroes subdued the last of the floaters or drove them into the burning water lifted his heart. The plan had worked! If not the war, they'd at least won a battle. Will clapped the big guy on the shoulder. Let him enjoy the win, while he was still able.

Rapt in his somber thoughts, tallying the human cost of victory, Will didn't notice the first drops of rain that touched the backs of his hands and sprinkled the roadway. But then thunder boomed overhead and the rain began in earnest.

Will looked up, his savage frown dissolving into a shocked O of disbelief.

"No, no, no," he said, shaking his head.

As the skies opened and the deluge descended.

13

THE RAIN LASTED THREE whole days and nights. Bazalgette's magnificent sewage system, unable to contain its fetid cargo, released tons of feces, dead cats and dogs, river rats and floaters into the Thames. Fourteen people drowned and hundreds in the low-lying districts of South London saw the mud reach the six-foot mark in their parlors. Beds were piled on tables, clothes and mattresses rendered filthy and unusable. In one home a chair was driven through a ceiling and hung suspended after the water receded. Sunday joints washed out of the ovens and the brick wall of a local convent was swept away. Outhouses, sheds and chicken coops sailed down the streets. The hospitals filled with patients suffering from bronchitis. And inhabitants were days at removing the oozy banks that shored against their homes.

By a lucky coincidence, the moon was at quarter and the outgoing tide greater than the incoming and the flood currents so fierce most of the floaters that survived burning were swept out to sea. Authorities and citizens remained vigilant and the bogles were chopped and burned as found.

But the London fires were extinguished, and an end put to the plague of living dead.

***

The front page of the *ILLUSTRATED POLICE NEWS* showed the Regent's Canal Dock ablaze. If anything, the illustration was less sensational than Will's memory of the actual event. He had been there and the paper, emphasizing wanton destruction and loss of property, failed to include the bodies, human and inhuman, that littered the quays and jetties before the night was over. And the newsprint that smudged Will's fingers as he read the text failed utterly to convey the reek of burning oil and choking stench of charred flesh that fouled the smoke-laden air that night.

The headline read:

HOOLIGANS DESTROY DOCK

The text below read:

"As fire ravaged the city and police and Her Majesty's army battled the plague of animated corpses lately risen from London's waterways, as well as legions of looters, and tried to restore order, hooligans from every quarter joined forces to set fire to the Regent's Canal Dock.

Six ocean-going sailing ships were lost in the conflagration, as well as four colliers and dozens of smaller craft. Of the Dock's warehouses, cranes, lumber yards, coal bins and oil tanks, all that remains are ruins, despite the deluge that extinguished the city's flames."

Will turned the page and read on. Momentarily, he looked up from where he sat in the private room behind the bar in the public house off the Walk.

"Says here some deaders washed up in Holland, caused a bit of a ruckus," he said.

"Better the Duchies' problem than ours," Kate said. The scratch on her cheek had festered some. Otherwise, a bath and a change into a yellow dress had worked wonders for her appearance.

Will had to agree. At least his city was safe. And if the plague returned, he had a few ideas how to deal with it.

He folded the paper, laid it on the table, rose. He removed his bowler and sat it on the paper.

"Give me a kiss, Kate, and wish me luck." He was dressed for the evening's adventure in a fresh white shirt and a dark-blue neckerchief neatly knotted about his neck.

"You make your own luck, Will Tagget. But I'll give you a kiss and wish you a speedy return."

Not too speedy, he thought. He wanted to savor the night. He handled the chopper in his pocket. The Lambeth Lads were off to the Embankment. They still had a score to settle.

"Don't take too long," Kate said and put her arms around him. "You'll know where to find me."

She gave him his kiss.

***

One good thing came of the flood: handymen were much in demand. At six in the morning a week past the flood, Ephraim Potts was bumping his pushcart over the cobblestones of Saffron Hill when a startling sight arrested his progress.

Set into the road at the intersection of Greville, there is a heavy iron drainage grate beneath which may be heard the roar of rushing water. It is the remains of the River Fleet, long covered over and turned into a sewer. On sunny days if you bend over the grate and peer into the gloom, you may discern the glint of the flow.

But what stopped Ephraim in his tracks was not the unusually loud roar of the water, but the fingers curled around the iron lattice of the grate. Grey fingers glistening and bloated like rotting sausages.

Shaking and resisting the sudden urge to pee, his heart beating like drums at the Queen's jubilee, Ephraim set down his cart and stepped closer to see what face belonged to the fingers.

Red eyes set in a pale and hungry visage glared up at him from within the sunken world. As Ephraim fled raising the cry, his cart abandoned, a roar of rage and frustration shook the dawn.

THE END?

Not if you want to dive into more of Crystal Lake Publishing's Tales from the Darkest Depths!

Check out our amazing website and online store (https://www.crystallakepub.com)

We always have great new projects and content on the website to dive into, as well as a newsletter, behind the scenes options, social media platforms, and our own dark fiction shared-world series and our very own store. If you use the IGotMyCLPBook! coupon code in the store (at the checkout), you'll get a one-time-only 50% discount on your first eBook purchase!

Our webstore even has categories specifically for KU books, non-fiction, anthologies, and of course more novels and novellas.

ABOUT THE AUTHOR

Garrett Boatman is the author of Stage Fright, a Paperback from Hell selection published by Valancourt Books. His story "Rain" appears in The Valancourt Book of Horror Stories, Vol. IV. Garrett's obsession with horror began with his grandmother's Bloody Bones bedtime stories. Later, a steady diet of Chiller Theatre and horror novels left him with a burning desire to contribute to the madness. A retired English teacher, Garrett lives with his wife Roberta in the hinterlands of Western New Jersey and may be found tearing through the woods on his bike when he's not writing.

Though the events in Floaters are fiction, the gangs were real. For more about London hooligans and the world of Floaters, visit Garrett at his website www.garrettboatmanauthor.com.

Readers . . .

It makes our day to know you reached the end of our book. Thank you so much. This is why we do what we do every single day.

Whether you found the book good or great, we'd love to hear what you thought. Please take a moment to leave a short review on Amazon, Goodreads, etc. No need to write an in-depth discussion. Even a single sentence will be greatly appreciated. Reviews go a long way to helping a book sell, and is great for an author's career. It'll also help us to continue publishing quality books. You can also share a photo of yourself holding this book with the hashtag #IGotMyCLPBook!

Thank you again for taking the time to journey with Crystal Lake Publishing.

Visit our Linktree page for a list of our social media platforms. https://linktr.ee/CrystalLakePublishing

Our Mission Statement:

Since its founding in August 2012, Crystal Lake Publishing has quickly become one of the world's leading publishers of Dark Fiction and Horror books in print, eBook, and audio formats.

While we strive to present only the highest quality fiction and entertainment, we also endeavour to support authors along their writing journey. We offer our time and experience in non-fiction projects, as well as author mentoring and services, at competitive prices.

With several Bram Stoker Award wins and many

other wins and nominations (including the HWA's Specialty Press Award), Crystal Lake Publishing puts integrity, honor, and respect at the forefront of our publishing operations.

We strive for each book and outreach program we spearhead to not only entertain and touch or comment on issues that affect our readers, but also to strengthen and support the Dark Fiction field and its authors.

Not only do we find and publish authors we believe are destined for greatness, but we strive to work with men and woman who endeavour to be decent human beings who care more for others than themselves, while still being hard working, driven, and passionate artists and storytellers.

Crystal Lake Publishing is and will always be a beacon of what passion and dedication, combined with overwhelming teamwork and respect, can accomplish. We endeavour to know each and every one of our readers, while building personal relationships with our authors, reviewers, bloggers, podcasters, bookstores, and libraries.

We will be as trustworthy, forthright, and transparent as any business can be, while also keeping most of the headaches away from our authors, since it's our job to solve the problems so they can stay in a creative mind. Which of course also means paying our authors.

We do not just publish books, we present to you worlds within your world, doors within your mind, from talented authors who sacrifice so much for a moment of your time.

There are some amazing small presses out there, and through collaboration and open forums we will continue to support other presses in the goal of helping authors and showing the world what quality small presses are capable of accomplishing. No one wins when a small press goes down, so we will always be there to support hardworking, legitimate presses and their authors. We don't see Crystal Lake as the best press out there, but we will always strive to be the best, strive to be the most interactive and grateful, and even blessed press around. No matter what happens over time, we will also take our mission very seriously while appreciating where we are and enjoying the journey.

What do we offer our authors that they can't do for themselves through self-publishing?

We are big supporters of self-publishing (especially hybrid publishing), if done with care, patience, and planning. However, not every author has the time or inclination to do market research, advertise, and set up book launch strategies. Although a lot of authors are successful in doing it all, strong small presses will always be there for the authors who just want to do what they do best: write.

What we offer is experience, industry knowledge, contacts and trust built up over years. And due to our strong brand and trusting fanbase, every Crystal Lake Publishing book comes with weight of respect. In time our fans begin to trust our judgment and will try a new author purely based on our support of said author.

With each launch we strive to fine-tune our approach, learn from our mistakes, and increase our reach. We continue to assure our authors that we're here for them and that we'll carry the weight of the launch and dealing with third parties while they focus on their strengths—be it writing, interviews, blogs, signings, etc.

We also offer several mentoring packages to authors that include knowledge and skills they can use in both traditional and self-publishing endeavours.

We look forward to launching many new careers. This is what we believe in. What we stand for. This will be our legacy.

**Welcome to Crystal Lake Publishing—
Tales from the Darkest Depths.**